"*I think we should be able to work something out.*"

Dallas chose a deliberately obtuse interpretation of Dexter's words and stepped away. "I hope you're not suggesting that I wash dishes until my debt to the hotel is paid." She held up her manicured hands. "I'd have permanent dishpan hands. Frankly, I'd rather face a night in the big house."

His mouth twitched, but he fought the smile. "I wouldn't think of calling the police on you ... but you must be qualified to do something."

Dallas sighed. "Yes, I am. I have my own business."

When she didn't elaborate, he waited. Finally, he smiled. "I have all night."

"I'm a C.P.A."

Dexter ran a finger along his jawline, and Dallas watched its journey with fascinated eyes. His body, his face, seemed more defined, more mature now. Dallas wondered if he was drawing the same conclusions about her.

She watched him uneasily. He looked like a man with a purpose, and Dallas wasn't sure she wanted to discover what it was....

Dear Reader,

June is traditionally the month of weddings, and at Silhouette Romance, wedding bells are definitely ringing! Our heroines this month will fulfill their hearts' desires with the kinds of heroes you've always dreamed of—from the dark, mysterious stranger to the lovable boy-next-door. Silhouette Romance novels *always* reflect the magic of love—sweeping you away with heartwarming, poignant stories that will move you time and time again.

In the next few months, we'll be publishing romances by many of your all-time favorites, including Diana Palmer, Brittany Young and Annette Broadrick. And, as promised, Nora Roberts begins her CALHOUN WOMEN series this month with the Silhouette Romance, *Courting Catherine*.

WRITTEN IN THE STARS is a very special event for 1991. Each month, we're proud to present a Silhouette Romance that focuses on the hero—and his astrological sign. June features one of the most enigmatic, challenging men of all—*The Gemini Man*. Our authors and editors have created this delightfully romantic series especially for you, the reader, and we'd love to hear what you think. After all, at Silhouette Romance, we take our readers' comments to heart!

Please write to us at Silhouette Romance
300 East 42nd Street
New York, NY 10017

We look forward to hearing from you!

Sincerely,

Valerie Susan Hayward
Senior Editor

PATRICIA ELLIS

Champagne and Wildflowers

Silhouette **Romance**

Published by Silhouette Books New York

America's Publisher of Contemporary Romance

For Kathy Coto,
For your smiles
For your encouragement
For your exasperation
For your friendship.
Everybody ought to have a Kathy in their life.

SILHOUETTE BOOKS
300 E. 42nd St., New York, N.Y. 10017

CHAMPAGNE AND WILDFLOWERS

ISBN: 0-373-08799-3

First Silhouette Books printing June 1991

Printed in the U.S.A.

Books by Patricia Ellis

Silhouette Romance

Sweet Protector #684
Champagne and Wildflowers #799

PATRICIA ELLIS

was born in Detroit to parents from central Mississippi. Being bicultural probably contributed to her wanderlust and love of travel, along with an incurable sense of curiosity. An actress at heart, she studied theater and acting at college, but found that writing came just as naturally. Currently, she is dividing her time between reading and writing romance novels and working toward her doctorate in Theater History at the University of Utah in Salt Lake City.

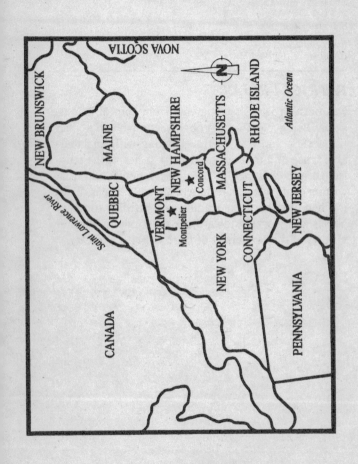

Chapter One

"I hate blind dates," Dallas muttered, slamming the car door. "Why did I let you talk me into this?"

Meeting her best friend in front of her car, Dallas paused, waiting for Kathy to supply some rationale for them to be attempting something so crazy.

"You're doing it because I'm doing a story on mail-order dating and because I'm your best friend. Someone you wouldn't desert under penalty of death."

"Oh. All right then. I knew there was a logical explanation." Looking at the elegant script on the awning of the Hotel Hudson, Dallas felt apprehensive. "But I still don't see why we had to come here of all places."

Kathy sighed. "Because the Hotel Hudson is classy and has the most subdued atmosphere in the county. We're less likely to attract unwanted attention in an elegant hotel lounge. We just want to have a quiet, informative evening with these guys without being interrupted every five minutes. Not that that's what has you worried."

Dallas's brow furrowed. "What's that supposed to mean?"

Kathy gazed steadily into her best friend's eyes. "You know exactly what I mean. Dexter Hudson inherited this hotel from his grandfather a few months ago and last month he took over the management."

"So?"

"So? So every resident in this city has seen him and most are talking about him. Have you seen him?"

Dallas knew better than to try to bluff her childhood friend. "No, I haven't."

"Dallas, I've never really known what it was about Dexter Hudson that made you dislike him, but whatever it was, it happened six years ago. He probably wouldn't recognize you if he ran you down in the road. You were only seventeen."

Dallas nodded. She knew she had changed. Not only physically, but emotionally. She wasn't the same girl she'd been when she met Dexter. What she didn't understand was her present reluctance to come face-to-face with him again after all the years that had passed. Kathy was probably right; Dexter most likely wouldn't recognize her now.

"You're right." She shrugged at Kathy. "Besides, he probably wouldn't be working this late, anyway."

Feeling the smooth silk of her dress beneath her hands, Dallas looked first at her own dress, then at Kathy's. "Maybe we shouldn't have dressed up so much. They might think we're desperate."

Frowning, Kathy glanced down at her azure-blue silk dress. It was a wrap dress that hugged her slender body and made the color of her eyes a brighter blue. "I think I look fine. You're the one who went overboard."

Dallas sighed. While her dress looked demure from the front, there was no back. The draping from the front cowl formed the sleeves at her shoulders and then fell to the base of her spine, just a few inches from being indecent. "You said it was fine when we were back at my place."

Kathy laughed. "I'm kidding. But you always were more daring when it came to clothes. Are you sure you're not a closet exhibitionist at heart?"

"I probably am. Either that or I'm just trying to shock people. Maybe I'm starved for attention. That's probably why I attracted the Neanderthal's attention this afternoon."

"What?"

"Oh," Dallas gestured impatiently. "There was a traffic jam on the freeway and this Neanderthal in a vehicle with those giant wheels tried to hit on me."

"How do you know he was a Neanderthal?"

Dallas's green eyes narrowed and one finely arched brow rose slowly. "He suffered from all the classic symptoms. Big muscles, smirky grin, arrogant expression. Totally unoriginal in his caveman approach. He leaned out of his car and asked me to write my phone number on his arm."

"What did you say?"

"I told him I wasn't aware that there was a monster truck and tractor pull exhibition in town, but that if he was interested in going to see a production at a Bertolt Brecht festival in Dartmouth, I'd be willing to consider it."

Kathy chuckled and shook her head. "I don't suppose he knew who Brecht was?"

Dallas smiled. "He asked if he was new wave or punk. By the time I got through about thirty seconds of my explanation of German epic theater, he found a break in the traffic and fled."

"One of these days you're going to realize that not all men who are hunks on the outside are stupid on the inside."

"I didn't say he was stupid," Dallas corrected. "On the other hand, he didn't demonstrate a real thirst for knowledge, either. I have a feeling he's probably my blind date."

Kathy sighed. "I hope not. No, I think that would be too much of a coincidence. Even for you. Now, come on." She had barely gotten under the awning of the hotel entrance when Dallas touched her arm.

"Wait, you never told me what these guys look like or what they sounded like over the phone. I picked John because he claimed he looked like Tom Selleck. You picked what's his name—''

"His name is Neal. Neal Baker. He sounded very nice over the phone.''

"I don't suppose that this John Hallett person sounded like Tom Selleck?''

Kathy cleared her throat. "Uh, no, but—''

"Nuts. I knew he was a jerk. Why did I even bother to get dressed up? And by the by...why haven't you shown me the pictures they sent?''

Kathy looked uncomfortable. "Uh, what difference does it make?''

Hands on her hips, Dallas stared at her friend. "All right, we're not going in until you confess.''

"Geez, what a crab.'' Pulling a picture from her handbag, she showed it to Dallas. "Neal Baker.''

"Not bad,'' Dallas commented, glancing at the snapshot. Kathy hesitated. Dallas held out her hand. Sighing, the aspiring reporter pulled out a small photograph and placed it in her friend's outstretched hand.

After a pause, Dallas spoke quietly. "This is a picture of Tom Selleck.''

"I know.''

"I mean, a picture cut out of *TV Guide*—there are program listings on the back.''

"I know.''

"You also must know that he's a jerk. Didn't you mention this when he called?''

"Now, Dallas, come on. It's hard to tell what a person is like over the phone.''

"What about Neal?''

"Maybe he's a jerk, too,'' she said quickly. "Now, come on.''

Dallas shot her a murderous look. "I got all dressed up for dinner with a jerk.'' Kathy ignored her sarcasm.

Dallas thought Kathy was looking forward with more than normal anticipation to her meeting with Neal Baker and doing her story. Dallas was dreading an evening with a drip named John Hallett who thought he looked like Tom Selleck.

"You know, Kathy," she said as her friend pulled open the door, "maybe I should have chosen someone else. This guy—"

"Listen, Dallas," Kathy said, her voice curt, "this is a calculated risk. That's what my story is all about. If John Hallett is a jerk, he's a jerk. Regardless, we leave in a few hours and you never have to see him again."

Dallas stared at Kathy's retreating back. "Well," she said meekly, "I guess you told me."

Two hours later Dallas was sincerely wishing she had chosen someone—anyone—else. As she looked across the dance floor at Kathy dancing with Neal, she tried to ignore the suggestive hand on her back. She also wished she had worn a different dress.

Neal Baker had turned out to be a very pleasant surprise. He had run the ad on a dare, not really expecting any interesting women to answer. Kathy had spent the evening talking about everything but her job. As she told Dallas in the powder room, "I'm afraid he won't want to go out with me again."

John Hallett, on the other hand, was a jerk, and certainly not a Tom Selleck double. What he was, was five foot eight without his elevator shoes, and he probably weighed 190 pounds. Dallas deduced that he had grown his mustache in an attempt to look like the actor. She also knew that he had failed. Miserably.

He was also obnoxious. Her pointed remarks about his resemblance to Mr. Selleck fell on unrepentant ears. He had laughed and made a crude remark about knowing what women really wanted.

Mercifully the song ended, and Dallas removed herself from John's groping hands. She had every intention of suggesting they leave when she saw Kathy talking animatedly with Neal at their table. As she sat down, she looked pointedly at Kathy, who was sitting next to her. "I see you're having a good time."

A sympathetic look was all Kathy had time to give her. John was leaning over to whisper in Dallas's ear, "I'm having a good time, too, baby. But I could have a better time if we left and went to my place."

Just the thought revolted Dallas. He had been making these suggestions for the past hour, and her patience was wearing thin. She leaned away from him and attempted a conversational tone.

"Do you go out like this a lot? I mean, having only seen a picture of a woman?"

John laughed. "*Do* I? When I see something I like, I go for it. That's what made me a successful businessman."

Dallas rolled her eyes at Kathy and whispered, "Yes, I suppose being the district manager for Speedy Carpet Cleaners must be just a few rungs away from the apex of power in the world of business." To John she said, "Can you get promoted any further?"

"*Can* I? If I play my cards right, I'll be regional manager by the time I'm forty-five."

"How nice," Dallas murmured. She had been listening to worn-out clichés for almost two hours. She knew his life story and was glad he knew nothing of her but her first name. She had insisted that Kathy not give her real name to anyone.

Dallas hadn't wanted to go with Kathy but knew her friend would have gone alone, and Dallas had decided that less treachery could befall two women together. But she had also had to consider her father and his reputation as a conservative congressman from New Hampshire. Kathy had promised to keep things low-key. Of course, neither of them could have predicted John Hallett.

"Listen, baby—" he began, placing his hand on her shoulder.

Dallas shrugged off his hand. "Don't call me that. My name is Dallas. Would you use it?"

"*Would* I?" John smiled. To Dallas it looked more like a leer. "Why do you have a name like Dallas, anyway. Were you born there?"

"No," she answered automatically. "Dallas was my mother's maiden name."

John reached over and grabbed her hand in a death grip. "Well, I like it."

She pulled until he released her hand. "I'm so glad."

Dallas couldn't stand this man. Neal and Kathy were growing uncomfortable. Dallas stifled a groan as she heard the musicians returning from their break. Kathy and Neal were up and gone with barely a word of explanation. John grabbed Dallas's arm and literally dragged her onto the dance floor. After one moderately fast number, John was perspiring rather unattractively. As the next number started, Dallas refused to be drawn into his embrace.

"Listen, John, why don't we sit this one out? Is that all right?"

"*Is* it? No problem. Some people tire out faster than others."

He didn't hear her mutter, "And I'm just about at the end of my endurance."

She excused herself to go to the powder room and was glad to find Kathy following her. As soon as they were inside, Dallas sighed in relief.

"Please let's leave. I'll crawl out through the window. Tell him I had a seizure and you had to rush me to the hospital."

Kathy was looking guilty. "Oh, Dallas, I'm so sorry he's such a creep."

Dallas brushed her chestnut hair viciously. "Don't blame yourself. You didn't raise him." Then she put down the hairbrush and sighed. "I'm sorry. I don't mean to sound like a harpy. But I'm ticked off. You and Neal are having a good time, and I'm stuck with the polyester king of New Hampshire and most of Vermont."

Kathy giggled in spite of Dallas's anger.

"I don't see what's so funny, Kathy," Dallas began, but when she looked at Kathy's face, she began to see more of the humor of the situation. "Oh, Kathy, I think I'll lose my mind if he says, 'Would I? Am I? Do I? Can I?' or 'Have I?' one more time!"

Kathy shifted from one foot to the other, and Dallas could tell she was about to suggest something that Dallas didn't want to hear.

"Uh, Dallas, I know John is a jerk, but..."

Dallas looked at her and could tell she was sincere in her concern. "What is it, Kath?"

"Neal asked me if I'd like to go to Garfield's with him to hear a new band. Since I know you don't like hard rock, I was wondering..."

Dallas drew a deep breath. "You were wondering if I would mind if you left me here to wrestle with the man with sixteen hands while you go and listen to some head banging rock and roll?"

At Kathy's apologetic nod, Dallas grimaced. "Sure. Why not? After all, I have my car. You leave with Neal. I'm sure John has his Grand Torino with the racing stripes and mag wheels out in the parking lot. I'll ditch him as quickly as I can. Maybe I'll even just leave when you do."

But John insisted on another dance, and ordered a bottle of champagne over Dallas's objections.

"Let's go to my place," he breathed in her ear when they returned to their table.

"Let's not and say we did," she said, attempting a joke. He didn't get it. "Listen, John," she began firmly, "it's been very nice meeting you, but I don't think we have enough in common to continue seeing each other."

There, she thought. Tactful and honest. Plain and simple. It should get her gracefully out of an awkward situation. Or so she thought.

"Come on, baby, you know I turn you on. You want me, too, don't you? Don't you?"

"*Don't* I? Excuse me, but I'm leaving now."

She turned to gather her wrap and felt his fingers close over her upper arm. He jerked her around to face him. His features were now twisted and angry.

"Don't get stuck-up on me, baby. I know what kind of women answer those ads. You've been coming on to me all night, and I'm not going to let the evening end without giving you what you want."

Dallas gasped and struggled to release her arm. "Let go of me, John. I'm going home now."

Refusing to release her, John picked up the champagne bottle and waved it. "No, not yet. I want some bubbly."

Dallas jerked her arm from his grasp and took a step backward. "I think maybe you've had enough to drink already."

Rising, John struggled with the cork. "No, I haven't. And neither have you. Come on, have a drink. Maybe it'll make you a little more friendly."

Dallas grasped the body of the bottle. "No, it won't. I don't want any champagne, and you don't need any more."

Not giving up his grip on the neck of the bottle, and still struggling with the cork, John continued to mumble about a few drinks loosening Dallas up.

Several people from nearby tables were taking notice of their barely subdued struggle. Dallas stopped pulling on the bottle but didn't let go. Leaning forward an inch, she whispered, "John, why don't you give me the bottle and let me call you a cab?"

The song the band had been playing ended, and Dallas saw couples leaving the dance floor. Soon it would be cleared. And they would become the center of attention. She could envision the disappointment in her father's distinguished face. What had he done to deserve a daughter who would answer an ad for a date and then fight with the date over a bottle of champagne?

Realizing that she wasn't responsible for seeing John home safely, Dallas decided to make a tactical retreat. "John, you can have the champagne, but I'm leaving."

She released the hold she had on the champagne, but John hadn't been listening and continued to pull. The bottle catapulted backward out of his hand and crashed into something behind him. The crowd gasped collectively. John looked over his shoulder, and Dallas heard his muttered obscenity and then silence.

She was aware of John leaving, but couldn't stop him or join him. Her eyes were riveted on the reason for his rapid departure. The floor-to-ceiling mirror at the rear of the dance floor was shattered, champagne dripping down it to a puddle on the floor.

Dallas couldn't move. She had always suffered from temporary paralysis after disasters such as this. In school Kathy had been the one who could run fast, having to haul Dallas after her. But now Kathy was gone, and Dallas could only stare.

Movement and murmurs from the dozen or so people near her brought her back to her senses. As she turned, she found herself staring up at two rather large individuals who could only be professional bouncers. She gulped and found herself being escorted between them to the manager's office.

As she walked along, her brain functions began to return and she squared her shoulders and held her head up. She had nothing to fear. It wasn't her fault. She thought about the possibility of getting away unrecognized, but realized the breaking of the mirror had focused everyone's attention on her, and there were at least ten people in the lounge who knew who she was.

But even the thought of facing her father with this latest debacle paled when she thought of the possibility that she might be brought before Dexter Hudson like a delinquent child.

He wouldn't see a certified public accountant who had recently opened her own office. He would see a postadolescent troublemaker. He would see a spoiled, pampered debutante who went around willfully destroying private property. And that wasn't Dallas Shelby. Her wish to avoid Dexter for the evening suddenly took on new dimensions.

She found herself in front of a door marked Carl Anderman—Night Manager. One of the bouncers knocked and opened the door, then escorted her into the office.

The man behind the desk looked as if he would rather be at home. He rose when Dallas entered the room and told the bouncers they could leave. Then he gestured at a chair, but Dallas remained standing, holding her evening bag and wrap.

"My name is Carl Anderman. I'm the night manager. Have a seat, Miss . . . ?"

"Smith," Dallas stated. She didn't know this man, and if she could get out of this unknown, everything would be okay. Mr. Anderman didn't look as if he believed her.

"Miss Smith. Now why don't you tell me why you found it necessary to destroy property belonging to the Hotel Hudson?"

Dallas didn't like the condescending tone in his voice. But with her options decidedly limited, she couldn't afford to antagonize him further. Casting through her muddled thoughts, she elected a plan of attack and hoped it would work. "I know this might sound bad, but it really wasn't my fault—"

Mr. Anderman held up a hand, frowned and sat down behind the desk. "You weren't struggling with your escort over a bottle of champagne? A bottle that subsequently broke our mirror?"

Dallas refused to be turned into the bad guy in all this, regardless of the consequences. "Well, yes. News must travel exceptionally fast in this hotel."

"We have surveillance cameras in the hotel."

Dallas glared at him. "Do you mean to tell me there were people in security watching that jerk maul me and did nothing about it? I noticed that while you apprehended the maul*ee*, the maul*er* seems to have made a clean getaway."

Mr. Anderman looked a bit uncomfortable at that statement, but he merely cleared his throat and looked up at her.

"Yes, well, Miss Smith, are you prepared to pay for the damages you incurred?"

Dallas planted her feet and crossed her arms under her breasts. "I'd like to finish my explanation. As I was saying, it wasn't really my fault. As a matter of fact, I was trying to avoid exactly this sort of disaster. If I'd known he wasn't paying attention, I wouldn't have let go and—"

"And shattered a five-thousand-dollar mirror."

Dallas stared at him. Five thousand dollars! She didn't have five thousand dollars. And even if she did, she wouldn't pay for a mirror that John Hallett had accidently helped her break. And she wouldn't let her father pay for it, either. Self-preservational instincts ran rampant for a moment, then she took a deep breath to steady herself. Responsibility reared its expensive head.

Acknowledging to herself that she was at least partly at fault, Dallas resolved that if she were going to be stuck with paying for the mirror, then John Hallett should pay half.

"Mr. Anderman, I don't want to fight with you about this. I know I am at least partly responsible, although I don't see how it could have been foreseen. But since it was my escort who actually broke the mirror, I feel he should bear at least half the burden of replacing it. The best I can do right now is offer to pay the hotel about twenty dollars a week until I can afford more. My personal finances aren't exactly in the best shape right now."

Dallas thought that was more than fair and was relieved to see Mr. Anderman at least considering her offer. Now if she could only get him to agree to it and get out of the hotel without any further trouble, she'd go home and crawl into bed and try to forget that the whole evening had ever happened.

Dallas moved away from the desk to stand before a plate glass window that looked out over the Merrimack River. Her thoughts were interrupted by the opening of the door. She glanced over her shoulder, but whoever it was didn't come in and was blocked from her view.

"Carl, what the hell happened to the mirror? I stopped by the lounge for a drink and—"

When the deep voice stopped, Dallas knew that Mr. Anderman must have indicated her presence. She turned to face the window again. *Trapped.* It may have been six years and his voice was deeper, more resonant, but she knew exactly who was speaking. Dexter Hudson. Dallas couldn't decide if she felt more like laughing hysterically or crying in frustration.

In the reflection of the window she saw Carl Anderman gesturing toward her. Then she watched as the newest character in this absurd drama entered. Her makeshift mirror was too hazy to make out his features, but Dallas thought that was probably for the best. What she could see jibed with what she remembered. Six foot three or four and at least two hundred pounds. Broad shoulders and a deep chest. Actually, she thought abstractly, he seemed bigger and tougher now. Of course, that was probably to be expected after six years.

One thing was certain—he was angry.

"That," Anderman was saying, "is what happened to the mirror."

Dallas could see Dexter looking at her bare back, and she turned slowly to face him. For a split second she thought he hadn't recognized her, but then he looked straight into her eyes. His tight expression became puzzled, and then he smiled and she knew he had. That smile hadn't changed. It still had the power to turn her insides to mush.

"Well, if it isn't Houston," he said, using one of the names he used to tease her with.

"Told me her name was Smith."

They both turned to stare at Carl Anderman. He looked confused and then cleared his throat. "It seems the young lady here got into it with her boyfriend and took it out on the mirror. It's all on tape."

Dallas felt like strangling Carl Anderman. "He is *not* my boyfriend! And I resent the fact that everyone is laying the blame for this solely on me."

Anderman went on as if she hadn't spoken. "She says she can't pay for the mirror and—"

"What happened to the boyfriend?" Dexter asked.

"He is not my boyfriend," Dallas repeated. All the reaction she got was a raised eyebrow. Then he looked back at the night manager.

"He, uh, left before security arrived."

"The creep gets away and leaves the victim of his lechery to face the firing squad," Dallas mumbled.

"I beg your pardon?"

Dallas was surprised he had heard her. She looked around and behind her and then pointed a manicured finger at herself. "Were you speaking to me? And here I thought I had faded into the decor."

Anderman wasn't amused, but Dexter seemed to be fighting a grin. Dallas sighed and faced the window. Let them have their macho fun. When they were ready to speak to her, she would explain everything. Besides, she needed time to collect her own thoughts. The fact that Dexter not only recognized her, but remembered one of the pet names he called her, was a surprise. She had prepared herself for his arrogance, his blank expression at the mention of her name, but never for a friendly smile. Actually, a little more than friendly.

She looked at the reflection in the window when she heard the sound of the door closing. She saw Dexter looking at her bare back again. She turned away from the window and walked over to a bookcase, pretending to be interested in the books on hotel and restaurant management.

She kept expecting him to say something. After two of the longest minutes of her life, she turned abruptly to face him. He was still watching her.

"Look, Dexter, I offered to pay for half of the mirror in installments. That's really all I can afford right now. And I think that's more than fair, considering the fact that it really wasn't my fault."

"I know. Anderman said your boyfriend was the one who actually broke it, but that you helped."

Dallas gritted her teeth. "He is not my boyfriend."

Dexter shrugged and sat on the edge of the desk, one leg swinging slightly. Dallas's eyes were drawn involuntarily to the muscle play of his powerful thighs beneath the fabric of his expensive pants. She quickly pulled her eyes back to his and silently dared him to say anything.

He merely smiled, rather mockingly. "Dallas, since you're the only one here, and you do admit holding the bottle of champagne in question—that is true, isn't it? You were holding the bottle that broke my mirror?"

Dallas nodded dumbly, and then thought, What is he, a district attorney? She tried to shake some of the fog from her brain and gain control.

"Yes, I was, but it was jerked from my hand. I have witnesses. Everyone on the floor saw what happened. Hell, you even have a videotape of the second round."

Dexter covered his mouth with his hand. Dallas didn't know if he was thinking or trying to keep from laughing. Then he picked up a pad of paper and a pen from the desk. "If you'll give me the name and address and telephone number of your date, I'll see..."

His words trailed off as he noticed the expression on Dallas's face. She backed away a few steps. "Um...well, I don't know all of those things. It was a blind date. All I know is that his name is John Hallett and that he's a district manager for Speedy Carpet Cleaners."

He looked at her as if she were a nut. Then he took another tack. "What about the person who set up the date? They probably know where he lives and his number."

Dallas took another step backward. She didn't want to tell Dexter Hudson the story of how she and Kathy got their dates. Unfortunately she didn't seem to have another option to explain her ignorance about John Hallett.

"Well," she began, "I'm reasonably sure she'll have his phone number, if he gave his real one. We didn't. John and I were with another couple—also on a blind date—but they left early." She closed her eyes to his disbelieving stare. "All of this could have been avoided if I hadn't had to make a point about a Tom Selleck look-alike. And if I didn't hate heavy metal music, I could have left with Kathy and Neal.''

As she opened her eyes and looked at Dexter's confused expression, she knew she was raving like an escaped mental patient.

''You see,'' she began again, ''Kathy—do you remember Kathy Roth? She writes for the paper now. Anyway, Kathy is doing this newspaper assignment on mail-order dating, and me, being her friend and the adventurous sort—''

Her tongue froze at the look on Dexter's face. He rose slowly and closed the short distance between them, then he towered over her. Dallas tilted her head back all the way so that she could still look at his face.

''You left yourself open to every crackpot and weirdo in New England. Do you realize what kind of a lunatic you could have gotten tangled up with?''

Dallas started to smile, but his expression made her smother it. ''That's what I said at first, but we planned it and Neal really was nice. It was just that I had to prove a point and pick the most obvious faker. I wanted to give Kathy some good stuff for her article. And all I ended up with was a pathetic jerk in a cheap suit who thought I was hot for him.'' She grimaced, but Dexter didn't seem to be losing his thunderous expression. What did he care what she did with her social life? It was just typical of the overbearing macho man she'd expected him to be. He thought being male gave him a divine right to make decisions for any female he knew.

She backed away and drew a deep, steadying breath. Now that he knew the whole stupid story, maybe he would let her go in peace. ''So, anyway, now you know what happened. I offered to pay for half of the mirror in installments, but that's the best I can do right now.''

Dexter continued to gaze down at her, his gray eyes boring into her face. He really hasn't changed, she told herself. He's still an intimidating, arrogant, conceited, muscle-bound Neanderthal. A Neanderthal with an Ivy League education, but nevertheless, a caveman.

"I think we should be able to work something out."

Dallas chose a deliberately obtuse interpretation of his words and stepped away from him. "I certainly hope you aren't suggesting that I wash dishes until my debt is paid. Do you know how many dishes I would have to wash to pay for a five-thousand-dollar mirror?" She held up her manicured hands. "I would have permanent dishpan hands. Frankly I'd rather face a night in the big house."

His mouth twitched in humor at her ridiculous remark, but he fought the smile.

"I wouldn't think of calling the police on you, but you must be qualified to do something."

Dallas sighed. "Yes, I am. I have my own business."

When she didn't elaborate, he waited. Finally he smiled. "I have all night."

"I'm an accountant."

"CPA?"

"Yes. About three months ago, after I became certified, I moved back to Concord to open my own office."

"Is that how long you've been in business?"

"Yes, almost," she answered uneasily. He looked like a man with a purpose, and Dallas wasn't sure she wanted to discover what it was.

He ran a finger along his jawline, and Dallas watched its journey with fascinated eyes. His body, his face, seemed more defined, more mature now. Dallas wondered if he was drawing the same conclusions about her.

He turned abruptly and went back to the desk. Whatever else she was going to say was lost. He was so big and yet moved with such grace. That came from the fact that he was an athlete in college. He still worked out, no doubt. She frowned. This wasn't right. She shouldn't be thinking about Dexter Hudson as if he was an old friend. She should be trying to find the quickest way out.

She stood looking from him to the door, and he returned suddenly and placed a large hand on her bare back and propelled her toward the desk. When he stopped but didn't remove his hand, she looked up at him. Staring into her wide eyes, he let his hand drop and turned away to walk behind the desk and sit down. Dallas could still feel the imprint of his hand on her back as she sat on the edge of the chair.

"I believe I've hit upon a solution for both of us. A way for you to pay off the cost of the mirror and a way for me to get something done, as well." Ignoring her wary expression, he went on, "As you know, I've only been managing this hotel for about five weeks. And while I'm not sure, I think something's wrong with the books. They seem to balance, but I've got a feeling something isn't right. The profit margins should be bigger. I'm not sure if there's anything wrong, but I do know that someone who knows what to look for has to look at them." His eyes never left her face as she digested this bit of information.

"Oh," she said. "Oh! I'm terribly sorry, but—" She jumped up and stood at the edge of the desk. He was crazy if he thought she would take on that kind of project for him.

"Well," he said, and rose to tower over her, "I'm sure you'd be happy to pay for the mirror."

"But I can't. At least not all at once. Look, Dexter, I don't think you realize what goes into an audit of that magnitude. I have a business. I have responsibilities."

"I know that. But maybe you could work on it part-time at least. Actually, I'd prefer it that way. If someone's been doctoring the books, I don't want them to know about an audit before we know who they are."

Dallas almost groaned in frustration. While she didn't doubt her ability to do the job he was asking, she did doubt her ability to work with him on a daily basis and retain her sanity. She doubted he'd changed that much. Maybe he would listen to logic.

"You know," she said conversationally, "that an audit on that kind of scale can be extremely expensive?" Dexter nodded but didn't say anything. Dallas continued. "And since, technically, you can only hold me responsible for half the cost of the mirror, you're only entitled to twenty-five hundred dollars' worth of accounting services."

His grin was almost lazy. "Provided we can find the infamous blind date and squeeze the rest of the money out of him."

"I'm sure we can find him," Dallas said grimly. "Maybe we could call Speedy's and ask for a demonstration." To herself she added, "They'd never find the body."

If he heard her, he didn't acknowledge the comment. "Tell you what. Twenty-five hundred seems like a high estimate for this job, anyway. If you finish it under that amount, we'll still call it even, regardless of whether or not we ever find the carpet cleaning blind date. Is it a deal?"

Dallas knew she was cornered. Dexter Hudson was determined that she audit his books. And rather than hang around all night and argue, and lose, anyway, she nodded. "I suppose so," she conceded. "And not that I think you'd tell tales, but I'd prefer it if as little of this as possible gets back to my father. He has enough to think about right now with his re-election campaign gearing up."

She raised her eyes to find him smiling at her. Very disturbing, she thought. Why did he have to look so satisfied about it?

"I won't say anything," he said. "And I'll squash as many rumors as possible, too."

Dallas nodded resignedly. "As long as you realize that I have other clients who come first and whose deadlines will take precedence. Oh, I didn't ask. Do you have a deadline?"

He shook his dark head. "No. As I said, I'm not sure if anything is actually wrong. But I was planning on hiring an accountant next week, regardless. And then, like a gift from the fates, there you are, busting up my lounge with a champagne bottle."

"Very amusing, Dexter. When do you want me to start?"

"Monday? Listen, I know you're probably tired and want to go home. Why don't we have lunch tomorrow and iron out all the details?"

Dallas wondered why she was even considering it. If she had any brains at all, she would run as fast as she could. But since she obviously didn't have the brains God gave broccoli, she found herself accepting his invitation.

"What time?"

This was insane! She could see that satisfied expression again on his handsome face.

"I'll pick you up at ten o'clock."

"That's really not necessary," she insisted. "I can meet you somewhere."

"Humor me," he said firmly, and Dallas just nodded as she gave him her address.

She found herself staring into his gray eyes and knew it would be all too easy to get lost in their depths. Again. She tried to tell herself she was an adult now and could handle any situation that arose.

Tearing her eyes away from his, she started toward the door, but for some reason she stopped as she reached for the handle. She slowly turned to look at him. He was standing just a few feet away and didn't seem at all surprised that she'd stopped. Nor did he ask what she wanted. He merely waited.

"I should have said so earlier, but I was sorry to hear about your grandfather. He was a wonderful man."

Dexter nodded. "Yes, he was. He thought you were pretty special, too. He wrote me when you won a blue ribbon at that horse show."

Dallas blinked up at him. "Did he? He was a big reason I won. He was always so sweet to me."

"Yes, he was a great man. The best I ever knew. By the way, what happened to your horse?"

So he remembered that summer as well as she did, Dallas thought. "I had to sell him when I went away to college. I hardly ever got a chance to ride him, and it wasn't fair to him."

"That's too bad. And surprising. At the time I thought you loved that horse more than anything in the world."

He sounded genuinely sympathetic to Dallas. "I did. But I learned that loving something—or someone—doesn't guarantee they'll always be there for you." Dismayed by how much she'd revealed of herself, Dallas hastily added, "But now that I'm back maybe I can save enough to get another horse."

Dexter silently gazed at her for a moment before nodding. "Maybe. I'll see you tomorrow."

"Right. Good night."

"Good night, Dallas."

Chapter Two

The dream was intensely sensual, and Dallas didn't want to wake up. Consciousness pulled at her, but she fought it. He was right there, bending over her. She was lying naked on a huge white bed, and Dexter was there, just above her. *Dexter?*

A cold, wet nose nuzzled her neck. Dallas blinked her eyes open and received her good-morning kiss.

"Oh, Morty, why did you have to wake me up?"

She turned her back on the huge black dog, but he wasn't interested in her procrastination. He put a huge paw on her hip and barked.

"Oh, all right." She threw the covers off and stood up. Morty barked happily and began to dance. At least Dallas called it dancing. She didn't bother pulling her robe over the pale blue man's shirt she slept in. She trudged through the hallway, the big black dog dancing along beside her. She walked through the kitchen and stopped at the back door. Rubbing her eyes, she yawned and looked down at Morty's excited face.

"Going outside is the highlight of your morning, isn't it?"

He panted happily at her and barked again. She scratched behind one floppy ear and smiled. Then she opened the door and he raced out, sniffing shrubbery and barking again at nothing.

She was drinking her orange juice and reading her morning paper when she suddenly groaned. What was she going to do with Morty while she was gone today for an indeterminate amount of time with Dexter Hudson? She couldn't leave him outside all day without someone to watch him. Her neighbor, a young homemaker with a two-year-old, usually watched Morty while Dallas was at work so that the dog didn't have to stay indoors all day. But Peggy and her husband and their daughter were out of town for the weekend.

Picking up the phone, she punched out Kathy's number. After seven rings, a sleepy voice mumbled something that might have been hello.

"Good morning, you ex-best friend of mine."

"Dallas! Oh, I'm sorry I didn't call last night, but I didn't get home until—"

"I don't want to hear about how great your evening was, Kathy," Dallas said, pouting. "Well, maybe I will later, but right now I don't have the time."

Kathy cleared her throat. "I really am sorry about leaving you last night."

Dallas raised an eyebrow at the phone. "No, you're not. Stop lying. But I hope you had a good time, because you owe me for this one."

"What happened?"

"I'll tell you about it later. Right now I need to know if you can come get Morty and dog-sit for the day."

Kathy paused. "Sure," she said slowly. "Why? Are you going somewhere?"

"Yes, I am. And I am leaving in—" she twisted around and looked at the clock over the stove "—forty-five minutes. What? Oh, no, I only have forty-five minutes! Can you come over here and get my horse?''

''Now?'' Kathy sounded incredulous.

''Yes, now. I can't drop him off, because I'm not driving.''

''Oh. Who is?''

Dallas put her breakfast dishes in the sink. ''I don't have time to explain. Could you just jump in your car and come get him?''

''I guess so. Boy, you really know how to ruin a Sunday morning, don't you?''

Dallas laughed. ''Since you ruined my Saturday night, why don't we call it even? See you in a few.''

She hung up before Kathy even said goodbye, then raced for the bathroom.

Twenty minutes later Dallas was furiously drying her hair with her blow-dryer held in one hand while she applied blusher and lipstick with the other hand.

Kathy arrived and let herself in. Morty bounded up to her, his tail wagging furiously.

''Hi, baby!'' Kathy leaned over and gave him a big hug. ''Do you want to come over to my house today? Whoa, watch the tail, boy. You're liable to break my leg.''

Dallas came out of the bathroom and began flying around from room to room, picking up newspapers and magazines and stuffing them under cushions, shoving her mail into the refrigerator and putting her dirty dishes in the oven.

Kathy stopped and picked up a letter that Dallas had dropped. ''What's going on? Are you expecting royalty? Who rates a clean house?''

Dallas suddenly stopped and realized what she was doing. Dexter. He was invading her unconscious. She had automatically been attempting to make a good impression. This didn't bode well.

''Uh, I don't know. I guess it was just that he's never seen the place and I—''

''He? Who he?''

Dallas frowned. "Never mind. I'll tell you later." She bent down and patted Morty's big black head. "Bye, guy. I'll miss you. Bye, Kathy, I really appreciate this."

Extending the letter she was holding, Kathy's blue eyes narrowed on Dallas's face. "What are you up to?"

"Nothing. Not really. And I don't have time to explain it to you. But I will as soon as I get back. I'll call you."

"Good. Now about last night—"

"Goodbye, Kathy. We'll talk soon. I promise."

Kathy backed out of the duplex with a frown on her face. "All right, I won't push. But I expect a really good story tonight."

Dallas waved as they loaded Morty into Kathy's back seat. "I promise you won't be disappointed."

Kathy rubbed her hands together in anticipation and started her car. She honked her horn as she pulled away from the curb, and Dallas waved at Morty, who had his head hanging out of the window.

A moment later a silver Porsche slowed to a stop in front of her. Dallas felt her heart skip a beat and then start on double time. She took a deep breath. Get a grip, she told herself.

As Dexter extricated his large frame from the low-slung automobile, she waved. He stood beside his car and grinned at her. His eyes dropped to her legs, and she looked down. She was still wearing her short terry-cloth robe. She was standing in the middle of her front lawn half-naked, and there was Dexter Hudson, enjoying it all.

"Criminy," she wailed. "I'll be right back. I swear."

She turned and raced back into her apartment, aware that Dexter had followed her. She pulled on a pink T-shirt and white overalls quickly, and then couldn't find her sneakers. She ran back into the living room, looking behind plants. Dexter sat calmly in an easy chair, watching her frantic search.

She got down on her hands and knees and felt under the skirt of the sofa. "Aha!" Then she turned and addressed Dexter. "Sorry, I'm almost there."

"Don't hurry on my account. I've got a great view."

Dallas knew he was referring to her derriere, but she said nothing. She grabbed the other shoe and then sat down on the sofa and put the shoes on. One of them showed signs of having been chewed.

"I have to have a word with Morty," she muttered.

"Who?"

The question was sharp, but Dallas shook her head. "Never mind. It's isn't important. I'm ready."

Dexter looked at her silently for a moment and then opened her front door. As Dallas passed him, she heard him murmur, "Yes, but am I?"

She decided it would be wiser not to ask questions. She locked her door and turned to follow him to his car. He casually placed a hand on her elbow, and Dallas felt her skin tingle at his touch. She frowned. As she settled into the front seat, she wondered if the past six years had ever taken place, because right now she felt as if she were seventeen again, and meeting a visiting college football hero for the first time.

After he had settled his own long frame behind the wheel, Dexter turned and grinned at her. Her breath caught in her throat. Good grief, this was ridiculous. She knew she was attracted to him, but couldn't figure out why. He was a Neanderthal. He was the first Neanderthal she'd ever met. He was also the first boy she had ever had a crush on. But that wasn't what she wanted to think about right now.

He started the car and steered it toward the highway. Dallas tried to concentrate on the passing scenery, the interior design of the Porsche, the air-conditioning vents, anything but the imposing man sitting so close to her. Every time he shifted gears his hand grazed her knee. She tried moving, but the interior of the car was so small that she had nowhere to go that wouldn't look as if she was avoiding him.

He was apparently content to leave her alone with her thoughts. She stared out the window and tried to analyze her feelings, hoping that by understanding them she could regain some control.

It was just a physical attraction, she told herself. One of those chemical things that died when you discovered that the object of your lust was a mental midget. Or a whale killer. Or a dog hater. Or he had no sense of humor. A lot of things could kill an attraction. And if she was really honest with herself, she would have to admit that she didn't know Dexter anymore. It had been six years since she'd seen him, and they'd hardly been more than friends—or friendly antagonists. So she really shouldn't have anything to worry about. She was older and wiser now and knew that physical attraction was fleeting. It would go away if it wasn't accompanied by emotional attraction. And when it went away, Dallas would be able to return her pulse to normal.

Now, as she watched Dexter from the corner of her eye, she found herself wondering if they had anything in common. Then she straightened her spine and scolded herself for her mental wanderings. Dexter noticed the small movement she made and looked at her quizzically. "Something wrong?"

Dallas felt like saying, *Yes, I've lost my mind. Would you help me look for it?* But instead she merely forced a small smile and shook her head.

"No, nothing. Um…what made you decide to move here and run the hotel yourself after you inherited it? Weren't you living in New York?"

He nodded. "Yes, I was. I was managing my grandfather's hotel on Long Island. He left me the Hotel Hudson here in Concord when he died. I've loved that hotel for as long as I can remember. I just wish—"

"He didn't tell you he was sick, did he?" she murmured.

"No, he didn't."

"I think he didn't want anyone to worry," Dallas reflected. "And he knew you would come and take care of his hotel."

Dexter just nodded and kept his eyes on the road. A few minutes later he pulled into a driveway, and after a few hundred yards, parked the car in front of the house.

"Here we are," Dexter said simply. He got out of the car and came around to guide her gently toward the front steps.

Dallas hadn't been paying attention when they arrived, and when she dragged her mind back from the fog and looked at the house, she stopped so abruptly that Dexter had taken several more strides before realizing she wasn't with him.

Standing before her wasn't an ordinary house; it was practically a Victorian mansion, rising three stories in places, with two chimneys and a wraparound porch. The shuttered windows and many gables had seen better days, but the house emanated a sense of well-preserved dignity.

She hadn't been to the house in years and wasn't really prepared for the memories it stirred. She'd always loved the Hudson home and had loved the time she'd spent here. Most of the time.

She allowed herself to be led up the steps and onto the front porch, through the double doors and into the house.

"I've been trying to get some work done on the house, but with everything that needs to be done at the hotel, it's been neglected," he offered. "I know you've been here before, but I'll show you around again and then we'll see if we can find Mrs. Foley and have some lunch." He gestured broadly with his arm at the entranceway. "You already know the foyer."

Dallas nodded. The "foyer" was two stories high. A huge crystal chandelier hung in the middle of the room, and a wide set of stairs led to a magnificent picture window in the wall above the double doors she'd just passed through.

Dexter nudged her forward and gestured to their right at several open doorways. "The parlor is through there, and that's the den. Down there is the living room." Veering to the left, past the staircase, he pulled her into the dining room. From what she could see the furniture was covered with sheets, and only some structural work had been completed in its redecoration.

"The kitchen and breakfast nook are through there." Dexter pointed, then pushed her through a swinging door and into a little butler's pantry that led to the kitchen.

Dallas remembered the kitchen, and this wasn't it. It had been completely remodeled and modernized. There were new appliances everywhere, and a set of antique copper pans hung around a huge butcher block and counter combination in the middle of the kitchen. A pan of soup was simmering on the stove, and several utensils were lying on the counter, but Dallas didn't see anyone in charge.

The breakfast nook was bigger than most people's dining rooms, but it had a homey atmosphere. There was a large round oak table and several country kitchen chairs in front of a large window, while several plants and a potbellied stove sat next to a fireplace. The setup had a sophisticated country charm that Dallas liked.

"This is my favorite room," Dexter said, echoing her thoughts. "So far, that is," he added. "Not much else has been completed."

Just as Dallas put out her hand to run it along the smooth surface of the table, Dexter grabbed it and they were off again.

They went back through the main entrance hall. As Dexter guided Dallas up the stairs and past the window, she tried to speak again. "Look, Dexter, you don't really have to—"

"Please," he said. "No opinions until after the tour is over. Now," he continued, "here we have the second floor. Guest bedrooms here and here, bathroom there, master bedroom and nursery at the end."

Dallas smiled as she doubtfully poked her head into each of the rooms for the two-second perusals Dexter was allowing. It was a classic Victorian house, with many small rooms that all seemed to be connected in some way.

"Dexter, you're not going to knock down a lot of walls, are you?"

He looked pensive and then said, "I don't think so. Why?"

She shrugged. "I don't know. I always rather liked all the little rooms. They were great for hiding in."

Dexter didn't answer but continued down the hallway. Just before reaching the end of the hallway, he opened a door and pointed at some stairs. "These go up to the third-floor attics and storage rooms." He abruptly shut the door before Dallas could see anything except the bottom three steps.

He then proceeded down the stairs with Dallas in his wake. They stepped into the hallway across from the kitchen, and Dallas noticed that the wall had several hooks on it. She remembered that they were for hanging coats and hats on when people came in through the back door, which was at the end of the little hallway. Dallas had just noticed the presence of a woman in the kitchen when Dexter spoke. "What do you think of the changes? At least the ones I've made so far?"

She fought the smile that sprang to her lips. "Oh, am I allowed to express an opinion now?"

Dexter looked a little surprised and then laughed. "I suppose I asked for that."

"Is the tour over?" she asked, wondering what could possibly be left.

He shook his head. "No. But you've seen most of it. The only things of importance left are the pool, tennis court and the stable."

Dallas nodded seriously. Naturally. How could she have forgotten? "Well, shall we see them now, or wait until after lunch?"

Dexter's mouth curved into a sardonic smile. "Are you sure you can stand the anticipation?"

She turned and walked through the doorway to the kitchen, saying over her shoulder, "I'll force myself."

He chuckled and followed her into the room, where they found a middle-aged woman making sandwiches and stirring soup. Dexter smiled at her with affection. "Mrs. Foley, I'd like you to meet my new accountant, Amarillo Shelby."

Dallas started and almost laughed at the innocent look on Dexter's face. His housekeeper merely looked expectant. "My name is Dallas Shelby. Dexter and I knew each other several years ago and, apparently, he hasn't gotten over his weird sense of humor."

The woman nodded and gave Dallas a piercing stare through her wire-framed glasses. Dallas was suddenly aware that she was being evaluated. The woman held herself stiffly as she looked into Dallas's wide green eyes, up to her chestnut ponytail, then let her gaze sweep over the casual T-shirt and overalls to rest on her sneakered feet. Dallas suddenly felt underdressed.

Then the woman looked into her eyes again, smiled warmly and held out her arms. "Miss Shelby, I'm so pleased to meet you."

Dallas was astonished. She found herself enfolded into the woman's embrace and wondered what she had done right. "Uh... thank you. I'm glad to know you."

The woman released her and began bustling around the kitchen, shooing them into the nook as she brought lunch. Dexter laughed as Dallas sat down, dazed and confused. "Sorry, but she does that."

"Does what? I'm still not sure what happened."

He shook his head. "Actually, you should feel honored. Most people just get the glares and a snub. Very few of us get the hugs. She likes you."

Dallas narrowed her eyes. "How long has Mrs. Foley been with you?"

"Me, personally? Or my family?"

"Both."

"She came to work for us in New York when I was ten. She remained with the family until a few weeks ago when I moved in here. Then she came to work for me."

Dallas was amused by this. "I can imagine that went over really well with your family."

Dexter laughed. "Oh, sure. They put up a fight, but Mrs. Foley always did love me best."

"Conceited little urchin," Mrs. Foley grunted, and hit Dexter with her dish towel after she set down the tray with their lunch on it. "I could tell you stories…" She rolled her eyes and lifted her hands to the heavens.

Dallas laughed and propped her chin in her hand. "Oh, yes, you must. I can't wait to hear about all the dastardly deeds he perpetrated as a small tyke."

Dexter scowled, but Mrs. Foley hooted with pleasure. "It would take more time than I have left on God's green earth to tell you all of them. But I suppose I could do highlights."

They all laughed, and Dallas leaned back and looked over the room again. A lovely floral arrangement adorned the table now, and Dallas stood and leaned over them, breathing in the scent of wildflowers.

"Oh, they're beautiful, Mrs. Foley." She almost asked where the woman had picked them, but she already knew. The meadow beyond the tennis court. She and Dexter had ridden the horses out there once. . . .

A smile lit up the angular lines of the older woman's face. She pointed out the window of the kitchen. "They come from the meadow behind the house. These things grow in abundance out there. I wasn't sure if you'd like them."

Dallas looked astonished. "Why? Why would anyone *not* like them?"

Mrs. Foley sniffed and glanced purposefully at Dexter. "Well, some people's taste in friends isn't always as good as it should be."

With that, she turned and left the breakfast nook to return to the kitchen. Dallas looked at Dexter and found him looking more than a little uncomfortable.

"Why, Dexter," Dallas said sweetly, "it would appear as if Mrs. Foley doesn't care for your taste in . . . friends."

He shrugged and looked at the wildflowers. "Mrs. Foley meddles."

Dallas smiled. "But you love her."

He looked quietly into her calm green eyes. He seemed to be trying to gauge her motivation for her question. Finally he nodded. "Yes, I do."

Dallas nodded and reached for a sandwich. "Then why don't you listen to her?"

Confusion spread over Dexter's handsome features. "What do you mean?"

She took a bite of the chicken salad sandwich and shrugged noncommittally.

His eyes narrowed slightly when she looked at the wildflowers, and he suddenly sighed. "Mrs. Foley didn't care for my former...uh...companion."

Dallas felt an unexpected pang of jealousy over this unknown person who had once been close to Dexter. She also suspected that *companion* was a mild term for the relationship. Then she told herself she was being ridiculous, but that didn't seem to change her feelings.

"Why?" Dallas said softly. "Didn't she like wildflowers."

He seemed to consider this before shaking his head. "No. She didn't care for anything wild. She preferred civilization and the city."

Dallas knew there was more to that statement than was apparent, but she chose to interpret it lightly. "Ah, I see. And Mrs. Foley is definitely country."

He smiled. "Definitely."

"Definitely what?" Mrs. Foley had bustled back into hearing range, bearing a pitcher of lemonade.

Dexter winked at Dallas and then shrugged at Mrs. Foley. "Uh...er...that is...nothing, actually, Foley, dear. These sandwiches are definitely wonderful. Yes. That's what was definitely...definite."

Dallas watched this strange performance with a mixture of amusement and bewilderment. She felt as if she'd come in on the second act of a play.

Mrs. Foley stood over them with her hands on her hips. "It isn't going to work, you know. I'm not falling into your psychological setup this time." As Dexter laughed, a loud raucous sound he didn't attempt to smother, Mrs. Foley turned to Dallas. "He used to pull this guilty routine on me all the time. I used to walk around all the time, wondering what people were saying about me behind my back. He's rotten to the core, he is. But it doesn't work anymore."

Dallas couldn't resist. "It doesn't? Why not?"

"I finally caught on to his little joke. I know he just puts on these little shows for my sake, hoping I'll fall into his trap. But I don't any more. I know he wasn't talking about me."

Looking up at the housekeeper, Dallas's face was solemn. "But we were talking about you, Mrs. Foley." The look of surprise, then doubt on the woman's face brought new gales of laughter from Dexter. Dallas ignored him and smiled up at Mrs. Foley. "But don't worry, because it wasn't anything bad."

Grumbling about ingrates, Mrs. Foley turned and stalked from the room. Dallas turned concerned eyes to Dexter. "She isn't really upset, is she?"

"Naw," Dexter assured her. Then, raising his voice, he said, "In fact, she's probably listening on the other side of the door."

Dallas heard a distinct "Hmmph!" from the other side of the swinging door. Turning back to ask Dexter if things were always like this in his house, she found him touching one of the wildflowers, a thoughtful expression on his face.

With a sigh he dropped his hand and looked at her. "Sorry, I was just thinking..."

"About what?" Dallas prompted.

He smiled. "Nothing. Actually, I should fill you in on the audit, which is supposed to be why you're here."

Any disappointment she felt at his statement she immediately squashed. For a moment she had thought Dexter was going to mention that summer so many years ago. When he didn't, Dallas couldn't tell if she was more relieved or disappointed.

That summer was a magical time for Dallas. She'd just turned seventeen and had gotten an adorable little car as a present from her congressman father. She and Kathy had practically worn the new tires bald in the first two weeks. They had driven all over the county, going to parties, barbecues, baseball games and drive-in movies. But mostly, Dallas drove it to the Hudson house, where her horse was stabled.

She had been training three days a week for two hours at a time in preparation for a state championship. And it was during one of her riding lessons that Dallas first met Dexter Hudson. He walked into the stable as she was grooming her Arabian gelding, Freelance, and asked, "Hey, do you know what you're doing, kid?"

Dallas looked up into the handsomest face she'd ever seen. "What?"

"That horse is pretty big. You aren't thinking about riding him, are you?"

Scowling up at him, Dallas instantly decided that looks really weren't everything. "Since he's my horse and I've been riding him for the past two years, I think I'll be all right."

"Kind of a little girl to be up on that big horse."

"I'm in therapy to conquer my fears."

He stared at her. "You're kidding."

"Yes, I am. How amazing that you noticed."

"Touchy, aren't you?"

She put away her grooming tools and began putting the bridle and saddle on Freelance. "Not usually, but then most people don't come around making stupid remarks like that. But maybe that comes from being knocked in the head one too many times."

"What?"

"You play football for Yale, don't you?"

Dexter gaped at her. "Yes, how did you know?"

"Oh, my friend Kathy and I go to all the Dartmouth home games and I remember you. It also didn't hurt that Mr. Hudson said you were coming to stay with him for a while."

"Of course. And here I was thinking you liked football."

She laughed at his sarcasm. "Well, you don't have to look so shocked. Girls are allowed to like sports, too."

He shrugged. "I guess. I'm Dexter Hudson, by the way."

"My name is Dallas. Dallas Shelby."

"Dallas? What's your middle name—Houston?"

Dallas rolled her big green eyes at him. "Give it up now, because you couldn't come up with a single crack I haven't already heard. My mother's maiden name was Dallas. Don't you recognize familial dedication when you hear it?"

"Sure." He looked quizzically at her for a moment, and then his eyebrows shot up. "Oh, yes, now I remember that name. Shelby. As in Congressman Shelby."

"Yes, he's my father. What does your father do?"

"He's a tycoon down in New York."

Dallas blinked at the absence of inflection in Dexter's voice when he spoke of his father. Having had a confusingly distant relationship with her own father since her mother had died, Dallas's first reaction was empathy. "I take it you and your father don't get along so well."

Dexter shrugged. "Nothing new. And it's not so much that we don't get along. We just hardly know each other."

Dallas finished tightening the girth on the saddle and started to untie Freelance. "Didn't agree on much while you were growing up, huh?"

"No, actually, we never disagreed. Mainly because he was never there. He and my mother are devoted to business and business trips. Always have been."

Dallas nodded, thinking that maybe Dexter wasn't as bad as she first thought. "My Dad's away a lot, too. Politics."

"Yeah, well, I learned to do without them. So did my sister. It wouldn't be so bad if they hadn't started interfering in my life."

Gathering the reins, Dallas smoothed her hand over Freelance's jaw. "What are they doing?"

Dexter looked away for a moment, then shook his head. "They don't like my choice of career. It took them until now—my senior year in college—to discover I'm majoring in hotel and restaurant management. For some reason they thought I'd want to follow in Dad's distinguished footsteps.''

"But you don't?''

"Not in a million years. My granddad is paying for my last year of school. Then I'm going to manage one of his hotels.''

"I thought he just had the Hotel Hudson here in town.''

"No, he has three others in New England and one on Long Island.''

Dallas was fascinated. She'd only spent fifteen minutes with Dexter Hudson, but she already liked him better than any other boy she knew. "Are you visiting your grandfather for the whole summer or just a few days?''

"I'm staying about a month. Then football practice starts in New Haven. I was hoping to have a little fun while I'm here, but I'm not sure there's much to be had. I should have expected it, though, up here in the boonies.''

Dallas bristled. "We're not exactly backward, you know. Concord is the capital of New Hampshire. We have—''

"Yeah, yeah, don't get so civically defensive. I'm used to New York. I'm not used to everything being so slow.''

First impressions, Dallas thought, are usually right. Whatever she'd seen in him that was interesting was now fading. He was becoming a jerk again. "Sorry to disappoint you, but—''

"Whatever. Listen, Houston, maybe you could tell me where the good hangouts in town are. How old are you, anyway?''

"I'm seventeen. And I wouldn't be of much help with hangouts, since mostly I ride my horse and work for the department of parks and recreation as a playground supervisor.''

"Seventeen? Whoa. That's too bad. If you were eighteen, we might have been able to have some fun, but I don't date kids.''

Dallas gripped Freelance's reins tightly and fought her anger. "I'm crushed," she said sarcastically. Dexter merely nodded.

"What do people under fifty do here for fun?"

She led Freelance out to the corral, and Dexter followed. "I go to the lake or to a friend's house when I have spare time."

"I guess I'll have to ask someone else."

"Good idea."

"See you around, Houston. Don't fall off that horse and hurt yourself."

Dallas seethed inwardly for fifteen minutes, wondering why a guy who looked so good had to act so dumb.

"And anything else you need. The office next to mine will be yours for as long as you need it. Dallas? Are you listening?"

Blinking owlishly, she nodded. "I'm sorry. What did you say about an office?"

Dexter looked at her for another moment before repeating himself. "I said the office next to mind will be at your disposal. It has a computer terminal in it and file cabinets."

"Whose office is it?" Now that she'd dragged herself back to the present and was grasping the conversation, she didn't want to displace one of Dexter's employees.

"Nobody's. It's supposed to be for my assistant, but I don't have one yet. So when can you start?"

Dallas tilted her head to one side. "I guess Monday afternoon. I want to continue working in my office in the mornings."

"No problem. I wouldn't want you to lose any clients because of me."

"What are you going to tell your staff about who I am and what I'm doing there all the time?"

Dexter scratched his jaw and looked at the remnants of his sandwich. "Actually, I've been thinking about that. I'd prefer they not know at all. That way, if something's amiss, whoever's responsible won't have time to cover for himself—or herself."

"Well, how are you going to explain me?"

"I suppose everyone in town knows you're an accountant?"

Dallas shrugged. "I doubt it. Since I just opened for business, I haven't had much money for advertising, and I refused to let my father introduce me to all his cronies. I don't need politicians and their weird money problems."

"So, basically, your friends and family know, but people who don't run in your circle wouldn't necessarily be aware of your profession. Hell, Anderman didn't even know who you were."

Dallas smiled. "I keep a low profile. I've basically been away at college, and I only spent Christmas vacations here in Concord."

"What about the summers?"

"I went to school during the summers."

Dexter frowned. "Why? Most college students want to get away for a while. Spend time with their families. Hang out."

Dallas shrugged. "My mother died when I was sixteen. And my father was hardly ever at home, anyway. Most of my friends were going to Europe or had summer jobs at camps or in national parks. I decided I might as well go to school. That's how I got to be a CPA so quickly."

"And now you've come home to Concord to live?"

"Yes. But what difference does all that make? Does it matter that everyone here doesn't yet know what I do, or even that I'm back in town?"

Dexter sighed. "I don't think you're going to like my suggestion, but hear me out, all right?" When she nodded hesitantly, he continued. "I think you should do the audit as quietly as possible, coming and going mainly by my private entrance instead of through the hotel lobby."

"But I'm bound to be seen by someone sooner or later."

"I know. That's why I think we should let people think we're having a personal relationship. That way, if someone sees you leaving or arriving through my private entrance, they'll just assume we have a date or something.''

Dallas stared at him. "You're right. I don't like it. Why don't you make copies of all the books and sneak them out to me?''

"Because most of the records are now in the computer system, except the hard copies we print out once a week for reference purposes. Only the records over ten years old are in regular ledgers. And the copying machine is in the main office, not my office. It would arouse a great deal of suspicion if I suddenly made copies of all the books.''

"There has to be a better solution," Dallas muttered. "Why couldn't I pretend to be your new assistant?''

Dexter looked at her patiently. "Because then you'd be expected to do the job of my assistant. And the people who may or may not be suspects in this would watch you like a hawk. And if you were my assistant, you'd be expected to work eight hours a day. And if you did that, when could you do the audit?''

"All right, all right," she said. "I get it.''

"You don't have to make it sound as if being my... er... girlfriend... would be such a hardship.''

Dallas closed her eyes. Conceited oaf. Just because when she was seventeen every friend she'd had had wanted to be his girlfriend didn't mean she wanted the same thing now. Now she would want... what? Did she want anything from Dexter at all? No. She refused to want anything at all from him.

"It's nothing personal, Dexter, but I—''

"At least think about it.''

Sighing in defeat, she nodded and rose, taking her lunch dishes over to the counter and wondering how he could even suggest such a scheme. Of course, to him, it was just a game. But Dallas was afraid that after spending that much time with Dexter, for her the pretense might become a reality.

Chapter Three

After stacking their lunch dishes on the counter, Dexter and Dallas walked around the pool and tennis court to the edge of the meadow. The grounds were still a bit ragged-looking, but she could see that much had already been done to improve the landscaping around the grounds. Dexter's grandfather had been hospitalized the last few months of his life and hadn't been able to oversee the care of his property.

They continued walking along an overgrown path that led to the stable. A large corral sat on the far side of the stable. There were four horses currently in residence, and Dexter told her a groom came every day to care for them.

There had been five horses besides Freelance who lived in the stable six years earlier when Dallas had ridden three times a week in training with Ted Barlow. Dexter had always seemed to be around when she was there, watching her, taunting her, making her nervous with his presence.

Despite her belief that he was a jerk, she had found her attraction for him growing. Normally she would have ignored anyone who tried to tell her what to do, but she had actually looked forward to arguing with Dexter. Except when it came to her horse.

"Hey, Waco, you'd better watch it on that horse. He looks a little skittish," Dexter had called out one day.

"I'll be fine," Dallas had muttered as she'd led Freelance to the ring. "But thank you for your touching concern."

"You're welcome. Do you mind if I watch you for a while? I'm waiting for someone."

Settling herself on Freelance's back and threading the reins through her fingers, Dallas sighed. "I don't suppose it would matter if I did object?"

He laughed. "Nope."

Ted appeared then and Dallas's lesson commenced. Dexter's presence was hardly forgotten as she tried to concentrate on guiding Freelance around the ring and through the mock course they'd set up. She wanted to impress Dexter, to show him she was good and, most of all, that she wasn't a child. Ted, a retired equestrian and friend of Mr. Hudson's, walked around the ring, calling out instructions on hand and foot position, speed and timing.

They were about an hour into her lesson when Dallas noticed a girl joining Dexter where he stood against the rails of the ring.

Doreen Handley. Recently Doreen had been voted most beautiful of the senior class of Concord High School. Her concentration split between her riding and what Dexter Hudson could possibly see in an airhead like Doreen, Dallas mistimed a jump and Freelance balked, sending Dallas flying over his head to land in the sawdust beyond.

When she finished rolling and regained a few of her faculties, it was to see Ted and Dexter peering down at her. Doreen was hovering over Dexter's shoulder.

"Are you all right?" Ted asked.

"Hey, how many fingers am I holding up?" Dexter contributed.

"Oh, I hope she didn't break anything," Doreen mumbled.

Dallas regained her breath and struggled to sit up, dismayed that Dexter and Doreen had witnessed her lapse. Ted was watching her, feeling her legs for broken bones, but not saying anything as he touched her reddened cheek thoughtfully.

"I'm fine, Ted, really," she insisted. She was flushed more from embarrassment than the fall. "Nothing is broken. I'm all right."

She got up and walked around the wooden fence jump to find Freelance waiting for her. Gathering his trailing reins, she stroked his neck and whispered in his ear, "Sorry about that, boy. I won't let it happen again. It was a momentary lapse."

"You're not getting back on that animal."

Dallas glared at Dexter. "Yes, I am. It wasn't Freelance's fault that I wasn't concentrating. It was my own. Now, if you don't mind, I'm going through the course again."

"No, you're not."

With that, he grabbed her wrist and dragged her from the arena, leaving a chuckling Ted and a fuming Doreen standing in the sawdust.

"Dexter Hudson, let me go. You aren't my father and you can't order me to do anything!"

Ignoring her protestations, Dexter headed for the barn, coming to an abrupt halt just inside. Dallas pulled, but Dexter retained his hold on her wrist.

"I'm not letting go until you listen to reason. And since your father apparently doesn't care or isn't aware of what danger you're in, I'll tell you. That horse could have killed you."

"Don't be ridiculous. I told you that I've been riding for years. Sometimes you fall. It was my fault, not Freelance's. And you have no right whatsoever to butt into my life."

Renewing her struggle to regain her hand, Dallas began prying at his fingers with her free hand. Dexter merely manacled that wrist with his other hand and pushed her up against the tack room door.

"Now will you listen to reason?"

"Reason isn't possible from a Neanderthal like you."

Dexter stared down at her flushed face, and his eyes narrowed. "Why can't you just ride and give up the jumping part?"

Staring him down at such close proximity was becoming more difficult as Dallas became aware of his long, muscular body pressing against hers. "I...um...jumping is exciting. It's almost like flying, and it's worth taking a few falls to feel...to feel the exhilaration of soaring over a jump with Freelance."

Dexter's expression softened a fraction as he looked down at her. "You need to discover something that's even better than jumping."

Missing his innuendo, Dallas shook her head. "There isn't anything better."

Lowering his head, Dexter smiled. "Oh, yes, there is."

That kiss was magical to Dallas. At first she was too startled to protest, or even to respond, but then Dexter's hands released hers and slipped down to caress her waist and her back. Her own hands found their way to his shoulders, and she held on as her knees buckled. Returning kiss for kiss and caress for caress, Dallas discovered sensual longing and pleasure in Dexter's arms.

"Dexter!"

The sound of Doreen's voice calling from outside the barn penetrated the fog they were in, and Dexter pulled away, staring down at Dallas's face as she struggled to control her breathing.

"I won't let you get to me," he ground out, his voice hardly more than a whisper.

Dallas stared, her green eyes wide with wonder. "What do you mean?"

He stepped back and shook his head, a smile of sorts playing on his lips. "Nothing. Don't you think that was more fun than jumping horses?"

Blinking in disbelief, Dallas felt her cheeks grow hot with embarrassment and anger. "Go to hell, Dexter Hudson."

With that, she kicked him as hard as she could with her hard-soled riding boots and took grim pleasure at his howl of pain.

"Ow! You little—what was that for?"

"I'm amazed you had to ask. But cavemen always were a little short on brains. That was for being a jerk. And, no, I don't think that was more fun than jumping. I prefer Freelance over you anyday, because he's more than just a horse. He's my friend, and he'd never treat me the way you just did."

Hopping around on one foot, holding his wounded shin, Dexter shook his head. "I hope not. They'd put you away for kissing a horse like that."

"Oh, why don't you just leave? Take Doreen with you and go see if you can come up with half a brain between the two of you."

With that, she turned and stalked out of the barn. But Dexter got in the last word. "Maybe I will. She may not be brilliant, but at least she's not dangerous."

Dexter left then, with Doreen clucking over his wounded leg. Ted resumed his position in the center of the course as Dallas walked over to Freelance and mounted, ignoring the sounds of Dexter and Doreen behind her as they left.

"Are you sure you're all right?" Ted asked.

"I'm sure," she assured him, clenching her jaw and willing herself not to cry.

"Good. Now that he's gone maybe you can concentrate."

"What's that supposed to mean?"

Ted started to smile but smothered it and scratched his jaw. "Nothing. Go through the course again."

And she did, without making one mistake. A grim sense of determination settled over her as she forced herself to forget Dexter Hudson altogether. Just because he was a great kisser couldn't overcome the fact that his personality needed major work. Freelance might not be able to kiss, but he was far and away more reliable and trustworthy a friend.

* * *

"Well, what do you think?"

"Hmm?" she mumbled, pulling herself out of the past.

"Maybe I should just wait until you wake up from your dream."

"What? Oh, sorry, I was just thinking."

He gazed at her steadily for a moment, then turned and gestured toward the house. "I was just wondering what you thought about the renovations I'm making to the house and grounds."

She walked back to the house with him and waited while he opened the French doors that led to the living room. After they both entered, Dallas walked over to the hearth and turned to face him.

"I think it's wonderful that you care enough about the house to do all of this. I always did like this place. But why did you show me what you were doing? What difference does my opinion make? What do you want from me?"

It wasn't until he raised an eyebrow and let his gaze slip to the swell of her breasts that she realized the implications of what she had said. She fought the blush she felt rising over her cheeks.

Dexter seemed to be fascinated by her discomfort. "I'd forgotten about that," he said, reaching out to touch her cheek lightly with his finger. "You're the only woman I've ever known who blushes so easily."

Dallas struggled for her composure. "Perhaps you've been associating with the wrong kind of women."

A warning shot sounded in her head, cautioning her against goading Dexter. He wasn't the type to listen without retaliating. At least he didn't used to be. Tangling with the man Dexter had become didn't seem very wise. There was a hardness about him that she didn't recognize. Her confidence slipped a bit, but she bolstered herself. Now was not the time to be vulnerable, especially with Dexter Hudson. As she racked her brain for something witty to say to lighten the moment, Dexter began speaking.

"I suppose I have been around the wrong kind of women, Dallas." His tone was a little self-deprecating. "I chose my companions carefully. I didn't want to get involved emotionally. I knew what they wanted from me, and they knew what I wanted from them. It was quite—"

"Boring," Dallas finished without thinking. She was seriously considering having her jaw wired shut. "Sorry," she mumbled without looking at him. The polished wooden floor had suddenly taken on a fascinating aura. "It's none of my business."

Dexter contemplated her briefly. "Perhaps not," he said at last. "But you're right. I *was* bored. Have you become bored with the relationships in your life? Is that why you haven't gotten married?"

Dallas's eyes were drawn to his. He watched her intently, and she knew he was probably trying to gauge her reactions. It was his purpose that eluded her. He was acting as though he were interested in her. And that wasn't something Dallas wanted to contemplate. She wasn't his type, and she knew it . . . which made his interest all the more suspect.

She shouldn't feel anything at all for him anymore. More than enough time had passed. But Dallas still couldn't deny the attraction she felt for Dexter, had always felt for him.

She didn't doubt he had had any number of "companions" in the past six years, while she hadn't been out on anything more than a series of casual dates. Dexter would probably think it was extremely amusing that Dallas hadn't managed to meet anyone who stirred her blood and heart the way he had when she was just a teenager. That would inflate his macho ego to the bursting point. Dallas didn't think his masculine pride needed any boosting whatsoever and chose to remain silent. Let him wonder about her social life.

She blinked, and his face came into focus. She was startled to realize he was waiting for her response. "Oh, I...um...I wouldn't say I've been bored. But neither have

I been moved to make a permanent commitment like marriage."

He nodded, smiled, then turned to pull the covers off two chairs. Dallas frowned over that smile. What was he thinking? Probably gloating over the fact that she didn't have a serious relationship with anyone and was afraid to pretend to be his girlfriend for a few weeks.

I'm not afraid, she told herself sternly. But he probably thinks I am. A determined gleam appeared in her eyes.

After they were both seated, Dexter leaned forward. "So, do you have any questions about the job or anything?"

"Actually, I do. Not about the audit, really, because I know how I'll handle that. But about this back-door plan you've got. How am I to know when the coast is clear?"

His gray eyes narrowed for a moment. "You're sure?"

"Yes. I think you're right. It's the most logical explanation of my presence." Silently Dallas told herself, *And it's also the best way I can think of to prove to myself that my fantasies were the result of being young and that, now more mature, I'd never fall for a Neanderthal, chemistry or not.*

"I think it'd be easier if we just met for lunch every day and went back to the hotel together. Some people may see you some days, but mostly they won't. And if we're seen together out and about, they won't think it's anything other than—"

"Yes, I know what they'll think it is. But really, Dexter, every day? Nobody eats out together every day for weeks. That seems more suspicious than—"

"Right," he interrupted. "How about we meet for lunch at different restaurants twice a week, and twice a week we'll meet here and go back together. Fridays are your own."

Dallas's eyebrows rose. "Gee, thanks."

"Hey," he laughed. "I think it's a great plan. And you'll be getting free food. And you can ride or swim if you like."

"Oh, no, I couldn't—"

"Sure you could. It's the least I can do. In fact, I insist. No need to be a drudge about the whole thing. What do you say?"

Dallas sighed. Why should she fight free food and amenities? "All right. But I do have a few conditions."

His eyes narrowed with suspicion. "Such as?"

Dallas rose and walked over to place her right foot lightly on the hearth while trying to sound brisk. "I want full disclosure of the books. Everything. Not just the books where you think the discrepancies might exist."

Dexter nodded and Dallas continued. "I'll continue running my business in the mornings and, if need be, I'll delay your audit if something pressing comes up with one of them."

Dexter didn't seem at all put out by her demands. In fact, he seemed a little relieved. She looked out the glass doors at the wide expanse of the estate. Morty would be in dog heaven here. She didn't see any reason why he shouldn't benefit from her invitation. He was cooped up in her duplex's tiny backyard too often for a dog of his size.

So, thinking about her big, funny dog, she added, "I want to bring Morty here with me when I come by."

"Forget it," came the terse reply.

Dallas swung her head around in surprise. Dexter was absolutely still, except for a pulse jumping near his jaw. His teeth were clenched.

She was almost afraid of him. What was wrong? What did Dexter have against dogs? She had known something like this would happen. They hadn't been discussing the matter for more than ten minutes and already Dexter looked ready to pick a fight. And over something as trivial as...her dog? Then she remembered—she had never mentioned the fact that she had a dog. Could he think that Morty... A thrill of sheer pleasure coursed through Dallas at the thought of Dexter being angry because of an imaginary lover named Morty. She almost dismissed the idea as too fanciful, but then she had to know. And a demon drove her to pursue the possibility.

"But really, Dexter," she complained, "how can you expect me to leave him there all alone? Especially if you're making me give up my lunches with him for you. He doesn't have anything to do all day, and I think it would be good for him to get out.''

''Doesn't he have a job? What does he do, sponge off you?''

At the dark scowl on Dexter's face, Dallas knew she couldn't go too far or it would backfire. But she couldn't resist just a few more jibes.

''Morty's lived with me for two years now, and I suppose he's very dependent on me, but I expected that when he moved in.'' She almost regretted starting this thing. Almost.

Dexter was quite pale under his tan and was staring at her with something close to malice. ''If you're living with this Morty person,'' he growled menacingly, ''why were you at my hotel lounge with that other guy?''

Dallas tried to keep her voice light. ''Oh, John? I only went out with him as a favor to Kathy.''

''Oh, yes, the journalist with a death wish.''

''Really, Dex,'' she reasoned, tracing the carved mantel with her index finger. ''It was no big deal. They weren't lunatics.''

''Is that why my mirror was smashed?''

She flinched slightly, but then rebounded. ''Your mirror was smashed because John decided I wanted more to do with him than I did. Some men don't accept rejection very well.''

''Do you always throw heavy objects at men who make passes at you?''

''Only the ones who aren't welcome.''

Dallas thought she had successfully drawn the conversation away from the threatening direction in which it was headed, but then she saw a shadow pass over his face.

''Which brings us back to Morty,'' he bit out. ''Your 'significant other' will have to wait until you're through here before enjoying your considerable charms.''

Dallas sighed. The fun was waning. She looked at the ceiling. ''Why do some men automatically jump to certain conclusions?''

A frown brought his black brows together. "What's that supposed to mean?"

Dallas looked into his hard gray eyes and wondered if she'd gone too far. She was afraid he wouldn't appreciate her little joke, which only proved her point about his oppressive nature. She cleared her throat and raised her eyes to a point around his hairline. But as she started to speak, her eyes were riveted to his again.

"Morty's my dog, Dexter." She had the pleasure of seeing him look utterly astonished. "Throckmorton P. Guildersleeve. You'd like him. He's overbearing sometimes, too."

Dexter slowly closed the distance between them and leaned against the mantel next to her. The mere proximity of his muscular body to hers sent sparks flying along her skin and set her pulse racing. And for some reason her brain wasn't functioning properly, because it wasn't sending signals to her legs to move. She just stood there, holding her breath.

Dexter raised a finger and just barely touched the end of her nose. "You," he said huskily, "set me up."

Dallas shook her head slowly. "You set yourself up."

His hand drifted down to rest on her shoulder at the base of her throat. She knew she had lost control of the situation. Dexter knew how he affected her, and with his thumb, he caressed her wildly beating pulse.

"Maybe so," he was saying. "But you knew what I was thinking and didn't bother to set me straight. You just let me believe—"

"What you wanted to believe," she finished, sounding more than a little breathless. "It was just a joke. What's the matter, Dexter, can't you take it?"

His eyes were suddenly burning with a new emotion, and Dallas recognized it instinctively as desire. She was afraid he could see it reflected in her own eyes. She should stop this now, she thought vaguely. But before she could organize her thoughts, Dexter was kissing her. And she stopped thinking at all.

It was a gentle kiss at first, and Dallas swore she could feel it right down to her toes, which were curling inside her sneakers. His lips were warm and persuasive, and soon Dallas felt a small moan of pleasure building in her throat that ended in Dexter's. She let her hands rest lightly on his shoulders for support, but soon that wasn't enough, and she slid her hands up to his neck, thrusting her fingers into his thick dark hair.

She felt him shift slightly, and he moved off the hearth, diminishing the height difference between them. She sighed with pleasure as they fit together perfectly.

He let his hands slide down to rest on her hips and then pulled her even closer. With a shock Dallas felt his arousal, and the thoughts that finally fluttered through her muddled brain were varied. She shouldn't be feeling this wonderful. Not with Dexter. Dexter wasn't right for her. Dexter hurt women like her. Women like Doreen were more his type.

Remembering Doreen brought Dallas back to reality, and with reluctance she withdrew from the sensual pleasure of his embrace and tried to stop the wobbling of her legs.

As her breathing steadied, she realized he hadn't put up much of a struggle when she pulled away, and was feeling a bit insulted until she noticed that his breathing was as ragged as her own.

Neither of them spoke for a few moments. They communicated far more with their eyes as they stared at each other. A lot had happened to each of them over the years. They weren't the same people now. It was starting to dawn on Dallas that Dexter was much more dangerous to her now than he'd ever been when she was seventeen.

Dallas didn't want to be the first to speak, certain she'd make a fool of herself if she did. Finally Dexter heaved a deep sigh and took a step backward. He never took his eyes from hers, and she didn't have the strength to look away. Dexter watched the emotions racing across her face, and he reached out and took her hand into his and tugged lightly. "Come on, let's go for a walk around the grounds."

Dallas nodded again. She didn't trust her voice yet.

He held open the glass door, and she stepped outside onto the patio and waited. He walked past her and she followed, not bothering to ask where they were going. It didn't really matter. And she didn't try to catch up with his long, purposeful strides, either. She just ogled his body from behind. And what a behind he had. She wanted to reach out and—

"What are you doing?" He stopped and looked around.

She shoved her hands into her pockets guiltily. Why didn't men ever feel guilty when caught staring at a woman? She then looked up at him with a defiant expression. "I'm not doing anything. Just admiring . . . the scenery."

He pointed to a spot just in front of him. "Why don't you go first so I can admire your scenery?"

Dallas blushed furiously at being caught. How did he know what she'd been thinking and watching? Good grief, not even her thoughts were her own. What was the point of pretense now? She squinted up at him, "Nah. I like it this way just fine."

He grinned as he reached down and grasped her hand in his, pulling her to walk along beside him. She smiled and looked out over the rolling hills of the estate. It really was beautiful here. She'd only seen it in the summer. Now she tried to imagine it in the winter with snow covering everything. It would be a fairyland. Would Dexter become a prince or an ogre? She knew he was capable of being both. Kathy had frequently admonished Dallas about waiting for Prince Charming. She frowned and tried to force the thought away. Dexter Hudson was hardly Prince Charming. He was usually an overbearing bully. An extremely sexy bully, but nevertheless, he was no candidate for princedom. Even here.

"Why did you decide to live here, Dexter?"

Her sudden question didn't surprise him. He looked over the open meadow and then back at the house, then looked down at Dallas's curious face. "Why do you ask?"

She sighed. Why did he always have to have reasons for everything? She looked around. "I know your grandfather left it to you, but...I guess most people with your career and background wouldn't choose to renovate and live in a slightly dilapidated mausoleum so far away from the nightlife and the fast lane." His expression was closed, but she thought she saw a flicker of something in his eyes.

"Is that what you like, Dallas Shelby?"

She stared up at him. "What do you mean?"

"Do you like living the life of the politician's daughter now? The parties, the money and the social whirl? I seem to recall that you disliked it as a teenager, but has that changed since you've...grown up?"

He sounded so cynical that Dallas caught herself just before she laughed out loud. She couldn't help but smile at his question, though, thinking of what her father or Kathy would say in response to that query.

"Did I say something amusing?"

Dallas nodded. "Actually, you did, but you didn't know it. Among my friends, I'm known as the party martyr."

He blinked. "The what?"

"The party martyr. I've acted as hostess for my father at his political parties and dinners since my mother died, but I hate it. So my friends started calling me a martyr for doing it."

"Why do you do it if you hate it so much?"

Sighing, Dallas let go of his hand and stepped away. "I've never been very close to my father. You know that. But when my mother died, I promised to take her place at those functions where a hostess is necessary. He was so lost without her. I wanted to help, and that was the only thing I could think of. I guess I hoped it would bring us closer, if only for a few hours every once in a while. But it didn't. Not really. He knows I'll be there for him, and he always says he appreciates it.... I don't know. I guess I keep hoping he'll suddenly want to talk with me and tell me all his troubles. I have a feeling he has many."

He looked intently at her. "Why don't you ask him to talk with you? Why wait for him?"

"I . . . I don't know. I guess I'd feel awkward or something."

"Maybe that's how he feels."

She frowned up at him. "Do you think so? I don't know if it would work."

"Can't hurt."

"Did you mend your fences with your parents that way?"

Dexter laughed ruefully. "No. But I haven't given up yet. Our fence has a lot of holes in it."

Dallas nodded, wondering if maybe he was right. She looked out over the field they were in and sighed. "So, anyway," she continued, watching him stare out at his house, "I could understand why someone like me would want to live in a place like this, but why would you?" He shifted his gaze to look at her, and Dallas suddenly felt as if she were being given a lie detector test.

"Maybe we're more alike than either of us thought," he said softly. He grasped her hand again, and before Dallas could comment he added, "I like it because it's set apart without being isolated. It's near the hotel, but not my family. It's a spacious piece of land in a crowded world. The house may be a monstrosity, but I think it would be fun to be a kid growing up in it. It's a part of my past—I remember spending summers here with my grandfather. I was always happy here."

Dallas felt curiously sad. It was a good insight into Dexter and his feelings, but she felt removed. She wished she could have something that concrete, that solid in her life. She lived in a duplex with her dog. She had a father she wasn't particularly close to and had no other close relations. She had a few friends and her newly opened accounting business, but now it suddenly didn't seem like enough.

Then she brought herself up sharply. She was a happy person, she told herself sternly. She had plans, ambitions. She didn't need a Neanderthal like Dexter Hudson in her life. He'd wreaked enough havoc with her heart to last her a lifetime. She'd have to be crazy even to have thoughts about getting involved with him.

Then she glanced down at their laced fingers as their hands swayed together. So why did it feel so right, so natural, to be walking along with Dexter? She felt a quiver in her stomach and knew her heart was beating faster than normal, but another part of her was feeling so serene. She looked around the gently rolling hills and wondered if it was the setting. She could smell the wildflowers and the grass, but Dexter's scent was more heady. It was subtle, a mixture of woodsy after-shave and something individually Dexter, but whatever it was, it was making Dallas's head spin. She was fighting the urge to throw herself into his arms and bury her face in his neck and just . . . breathe.

Her errant thoughts made her knees weak, and she stumbled slightly. Dexter's hand tightened around hers to steady her. She was embarrassed. Looking at the ground, she could see there was nothing there. Nothing to trip on. She gazed up at him sheepishly, planning on apologizing, but the words died on her lips as she looked into gray eyes that burned with desire. She swallowed with difficulty. And then her hands were sliding up his chest without her brain's permission.

His arms snaked around her, and she was suddenly crushed to him, her soft breasts flattened against his hard chest. But she didn't notice. He was kissing her again. And this time he wasn't holding back. Dallas felt her senses reeling. Then he pulled away and began nibbling on her neck and ear. Dallas just buried her face at the base of his neck.

Inhaling deeply, she couldn't separate the sensations bombarding her. Her skin burned where Dexter's lips touched her, but she couldn't control her own need to taste him, and let her lips settle on his chest where his shirt was open. When her tongue darted out and touched his bare skin, she heard him groan as he wrenched away from her.

"God, not now!"

Dallas blinked in confusion when she heard Mrs. Foley's voice carrying across the meadow.

"Dexter!"

They stepped away from each other. Dallas felt shaken, her nerves screaming in protest.

Mrs. Foley stood on the kitchen porch, waving at them. "Telephone!"

Dexter frowned and turned toward the house. Dallas followed him, but his long legs got him there ahead of her, and he disappeared inside. It was just as well, because she needed the extra time to compose herself. She refused to try to analyze what was happening now—it was too monumental a task. Especially when she was probably reading more into it than was actually there. In the kitchen she found Mrs. Foley waiting with brownies and milk.

"I hope you're not one of those girls who's always on a diet," she warned.

Dallas smiled. "No. I feel that as long as I exercise and don't gorge like a hog, I'll be all right."

Mrs. Foley chuckled and nodded. "That's right. And there's plenty to do around here. Tennis and swimming. Riding if you're the fearless type. Just walking around the yard is enough to tucker a body out."

Dallas laughed and bit into a brownie. "Mmm, this is great."

The housekeeper beamed. "They're Dexter's favorite. Do you bake?"

Dallas nodded. "I don't cook very well, but I bake up a storm. As long as people don't mind dessert all the time, I'm a great cook."

"Aw, you're just fooling."

"Well," she conceded, "I can cook breakfast all right, and I can make a sandwich, but after that it gets pretty ugly."

As the two women sat laughing and talking, they didn't hear the approach of the master of the house. Dallas was just finishing relating a story of kitchen disaster number seventeen when she looked up and caught Dexter leaning in the doorway, watching and listening.

"I didn't know you were an eavesdropper," she said.

Mrs. Foley rose and went over to him, giving him a brownie. "Oh, my yes. He's the sneakiest devil the Lord ever put on the earth. As quiet as a mouse and twice as mean. Nearly killed me I don't know how many times, sneaking up behind me and grabbing me. It's a wonder my poor old heart didn't give out long ago."

Dexter wolfed down the brownie. "Your heart's as strong as it was when you were twenty."

Mrs. Foley sniffed. "Maybe. But my not having an attack isn't for want of you trying."

He leaned down and kissed her on the cheek. Mrs. Foley beamed and patted his shoulder.

"Foley, dear," he said, "we have to go. The reservations computer at the hotel went down and all the employees are at sixes and sevens. I have to go and help sort through everything."

They left, and on the return to her house they arranged to meet for lunch at a restaurant on Monday.

As Dallas watched Dexter pull away from the curb, she wondered if she was getting herself involved in something that would prove far more painful than she had thought possible.

Chapter Four

Eight o'clock Monday morning found Dallas already at her office, located in a renovated building in the downtown area. It pained her to have to admit it, but Dexter Hudson's intrusion upon her professional life was hardly an inconvenience. She was easily able to fit Dexter into her schedule—having opened for business only two months earlier, Dallas was just beginning to get a client list started. At first most of her clients had been friends and relatives, but gradually word of mouth was beginning to bring in a few new people. Not quickly enough to make her rich, but Dallas was enjoying her career and was able to pay her bills, so she considered herself successful.

Now Dexter Hudson had given her what she would have considered a dream job just a week ago. But without remuneration it didn't taste nearly as sweet to Dallas.

Hearing the front door open, Dallas rose and walked to the doorway of her tiny office. "Morning, Cheryl."

A scream answered her. Cheryl Carlson, Dallas's part-time receptionist and only employee, lost her grip on her purse and dropped to a crouch.

Dallas started in surprise. "It's only me!"

Cheryl's tensed shoulders dropped when she recognized Dallas. "Good grief, you almost scared me witless. What are you doing here so early? It's not even nine o'clock."

"I have a lot to do. But before we get into it I must compliment you on your self-defense pose. Very impressive."

Her receptionist was taking a course in self-defense at the community center. Now she beamed. "Hey, yeah, it works. Reflexes. My instructor will be proud."

"And so should you be. Now let's go sit down for a few minutes in my office. I have some things I need to talk over with you."

Curiosity gleaming in her brown eyes, Cheryl picked up her purse and followed Dallas. "What's going on?"

"I've been wondering that myself, Cheryl. This weekend will have to go down in my personal history as one of the more disastrous in my life."

"What happened?"

Dallas sat down behind her desk and leaned forward, her elbows on her blotter. "I went on a blind date and wound up having to audit Dexter Hudson's books because of a broken mirror."

Staring at her employer, Cheryl only nodded. "Uh-huh. You want to discuss quantum physics now?"

Laughing, Dallas rolled her eyes. "Sorry. I guess I left out some of the details." She then recapped the events of the past two days, leaving out certain personal items that, while of great possible interest to Cheryl, were better left as private memories. She hadn't come to grips with her treacherous emotions herself yet, and wasn't ready to share them with anyone.

"Wow," Cheryl breathed when Dallas finished her story. "I saw Dexter Hudson about a week ago. He was at the bank. He's so...so..."

"Isn't he just?" Dallas shook her head. "But regardless of Dexter we have to get this place organized so that I can start work on his books this afternoon."

Cheryl grinned. "That should take about five minutes. We haven't exactly been having a rush lately."

"I know." Dallas grimaced. "But I still need you to re-schedule any afternoon appointments. Shift them to the mornings. And if any new client happens to call, do the same."

Nodding easily, Cheryl leaned forward. "No problem. Now tell me the parts you left out." Dallas's head jerked up. "Aha! So, you are hiding something. What did he do—make a pass at you?"

Dallas shooed Cheryl out of her office. "Get back to work, slave."

"Did you make a pass at him? Was there physical contact of any kind? Tell me—I'm starved for juicy tidbits."

Fighting a grin, Dallas shook her head. "No. Get your cheap thrills elsewhere."

Cheryl looked at her smugly. "Never mind. You've just told me more by not telling me anything than you would have if you'd told me everything."

"When I figure out what you just said, I'll come up with a biting reply," Dallas replied.

Her receptionist merely nodded at her. "Sure, boss. Anything you say. Will that be all?"

"I think so. Oh, you know I trust you, but please don't say anything about this to anyone. Dexter wants this audit done as quietly as possible. If anyone asks why I'm spending so much time with him at the hotel, just—"

"I'll tell them it's none of their business how you choose to spend your time."

Dallas shook her head and muttered to herself, "I'm sure that will accomplish Dexter's gossip goal."

After finishing what little outstanding paperwork she had, Dallas picked up the phone and called the newspaper. She knew that Kathy was worried and curious about Dallas's mysterious Sunday meeting, and she hadn't felt like talking when she picked Morty up.

"Feature desk, Kathy Roth."

"Hi, Kath. It's me."

"Dallas! How about lunch? I've got a lot to tell you."

"Sorry, I can't. I'm having lunch with Dexter."

The ensuing pause made Dallas smile, but she didn't say anything.

Finally Kathy cleared her throat. "Dexter? I thought Dexter Hudson was the scum on the pond of life, the personification of all that is undesirable in American manhood."

"I never said any of that...exactly. Besides, it's really more of a business meeting."

"Sure," her friend scoffed. "I don't want to butt in where I don't belong, but what's going on between you two?"

Dallas sighed and told Kathy everything that had happened. The more she retold the story, the more surreal it sounded.

Kathy was dumbstruck for about two seconds. "Dallas, what's going on? Is Dexter interested in you? And more importantly, are you now interested in him? Did he say anything to disabuse you of the thought that he's a male chauvinist pig? Has he mentioned the past at all?"

Dallas twirled the telephone cord around her fingers. "Uh, no, not exactly. We've been sort of skating the edges."

"Why is that? Are you afraid of the thin ice covering the deepest part of the pond?"

"Very good. Why don't you write that one down?"

"I might." Kathy sighed. "Look, Dallas, it isn't that I don't think you know what you're doing, but I do know that way back when you hated Dexter Hudson. You claimed he was a Neanderthal, an arrogant, male chauvinist without a shred of sensitivity or sincerity in him. At least that's how I remember it. Am I wrong? Or has Dexter's personality changed that much?"

Dallas paused, remembering how easily Dexter had always managed to manipulate her emotions. "Actually, I think it's probably a little of both. While he was arrogant and more than a little chauvinistic, I think my anger and confusion may have painted him a little darker than he was. As for now, I'm not sure if he's changed or not. Sometimes

I think he has, and then he'll say or do something that convinces me he hasn't.''

"Like what?''

"Oh, it's more his air of superiority than anything specific. The air of supreme confidence in his own masculine appeal still rankles me. He always gets what he wants, especially from women, because they're so swayed by his looks, not to mention his charm, which is probably manufactured.''

Dallas didn't have to tell Kathy that she herself was guilty of falling for that manufactured charm—she heard her friend's ponderous humming over the telephone wire. Kathy wasn't a reporter for nothing. When she got a hunch, she tracked it down and worried over it until satisfied. And right now she sounded as if she'd discovered a scoop. "I think you've been holding out on me for quite a while.''

Dallas tried to bluff. "What do you mean?''

"I mean, there must have been things happening that summer I wasn't aware of. Dexter made you angry, but anger wasn't the only emotion he aroused in you, was it?''

Dallas was at a loss for words. Then she knew denials were useless. "So I thought he was too intelligent and good-looking to be wasting his time on girls like Doreen Handley.''

Kathy laughed. "Oh, yeah. Doreen's handy. She just got divorced again, you know. This makes three. I'd almost forgotten that she and Dexter went out together.''

"Yes. Although she wasn't the only girl he went out with that summer.''

"Sure she was,'' Kathy said. "Their names and faces changed, but they were all basically Doreen. Did you secretly wish it was you he was going out with?''

"Maybe,'' Dallas admitted. "I was a teenager and he was a football jock from Yale. He was very charming when he wasn't being a Neanderthal.''

"And now you're not a teenager and he's still charming. And still a Neanderthal?''

Dallas paused. "I don't know. Maybe. I haven't figured out who he is now. He's not as predictable as he once was."

"Oh-oh. You're not going to do this all over again, are you?"

"No, I'm not," Dallas denied. "For one thing, I'm not as young and gullible as I was then. I've grown up and I know the difference between infatuation and love."

"Do you?"

Dallas sighed. "Yes, I do. And don't think I've fallen at Dexter's feet, because I haven't. I'm not at all sure he's changed that much. I can't deny he's an attractive man, but I'm trying to be rational and objective about everything."

"If you say so."

"I do. Now what was it you wanted to tell me?"

"What? Oh!" It took Kathy a moment to catch up with the change of subject. "My article on dating has been given the cover of the Sunday magazine, one month hence. And," she added dramatically when Dallas began to congratulate her, "Neal Baker called and asked me out again."

"Sure," Dallas moaned good-naturedly. "You find a nice guy to play footsie with you and I get caught in the act of vandalism, trying to discourage a jerk. Do you detect a discrepancy in the balance of luck here?"

Kathy laughed. "Sure do, but since I'm on the good-luck end, I'm hardly going to say I wish it hadn't happened."

Dallas scowled. "That's true, but the fact that I now have to go to Dexter Hudson's hotel and do an audit—gratis—just doesn't seem fair. I don't suppose you've been able to track down John Hallett?"

"No, but I'm still on it. I'm calling all the Speedy Carpet Cleaners in the state. But at least he's not here in Concord."

"Praise the Lord for small favors. Listen, Kath, I have to go. Please make sure no one finds out about the audit. The only people who know are Dexter, me, you and Cheryl."

"Don't worry about me. I may be a good reporter, but I'm a better friend. Besides, when it's all over, there may be an exclusive in it for me that might just get me a promotion."

Dallas laughed. "That's my altruistic pal."

"Ever faithful. Take it easy, and don't get in over your head with you know who. Call me, especially if anything interesting happens."

At one o'clock Dallas walked into a small family-style restaurant that she and Dexter had agreed upon. He was waiting for her, and after they ordered, he asked her if she'd had any troubles freeing up her afternoons.

"Not really," she admitted. "To be honest about it, doing this for you will hardly cause me any trouble at all." *At least professionally,* she added to herself. *Personally I'm not so sure.*

"So what do you do now that you don't ride anymore?"

Dallas blinked at him. "I still ride when I get a chance. I just don't train and compete the way I used to."

"Would you like to?"

"I guess so. I haven't really thought about it lately. But it won't be possible until I build up my business some more."

Dexter nodded and munched on a breadstick. "And in the meantime, what do you do for fun? Besides going on kamikaze blind dates?"

"Still a master of wit, I see," Dallas murmured. "Actually, I haven't been involved in much since I got back to Concord. I've been too busy setting up my office and getting reacquainted with old friends. What have you done for fun since you moved to Concord?"

He smiled at her mocking question. "As if I've had any spare time. Between getting my grandfather's estate settled and my family calmed down—"

"Calmed down?" Dallas asked. "Why did you have to calm them down?"

"My grandfather left everything to me, and that didn't sit too well with my parents. Not that they need the money or anything, but it was a little too much like my grandfather having the final word on how much he disliked their life-style.''

Dallas smiled, remembering the elderly Mr. Hudson and how nice he was to her. "What was wrong with their life-style? Too extravagant?"

"Among other things. My grandfather had a strong work ethic, and it ticked him off that my dad delegated so much authority and went on so many business trips. Especially since the business trips somehow all ended up being in the Bahamas or the Mediterranean or Hawaii. He thought people ought to work for what they get."

"And did you calm them down?"

Dexter chuckled. "I did just the opposite at first. I gave my sister the hotel on Long Island that I used to manage. Holly was happy as a clam until my parents started moaning. We all got together last month down in New York and tried to iron everything out."

Dallas watched him as the waitress took their empty plates away. He had been through quite a bit of stress in the past few months, and now he was faced with the possibility of an embezzler. She admired his inner strength.

"Were you successful? I mean, did you get everything worked out?"

"It wasn't a fun-filled weekend. But at least there aren't as many problems. I think Holly resents their interference as much as I do. They practically ignored us when we were growing up, but now they want to try and run our lives. I suspect they were peeved when Holly and I grew up more like our grandfather than them. Which shouldn't have surprised them, since he cared more for us than they seemed to." He looked at his watch and sighed. "Sorry. I didn't mean to go on and on about my boring family problems."

Dallas laughed. "Better your family than mine. And they're far from boring. Just remember to warn me if they ever come to town."

Dexter laughed, somewhat grimly.

When they left the restaurant, they got into their cars and drove to the hotel. Dexter parked in the nearby lot, and

Dallas parked on the residential street behind it. Two cars didn't give a lot of credence to the story they'd concocted.

Meeting Dexter at the edge of the parking lot, which was bordered by six-foot hedges, Dallas saw the unmarked path that led to Dexter's office. The area wasn't well traveled, since the employees' entrance was on the other side of the hotel and the lobby was in the front. No one saw them enter his office.

Shutting the door behind him, Dexter locked it. "Now," he said briskly, "this is my office. Yours is through here."

Striding over to a door in the right wall, he opened it and gestured for Dallas to follow him. He flipped on the light, and Dallas saw an ordinary office. A bit on the small side but comfortable-looking, it had a nice wooden desk, a swivel chair, a file cabinet, a typewriter, a typing table and a computer terminal.

"I'll see about getting you another chair," he told her.

Dallas shrugged. "What for? I only have one—er, that is, I only need one to sit on."

Chuckling softly, Dexter nodded. "Yes, I know, but I may have to visit your office from time to time."

She nodded lamely, wondering how much time he planned on spending with her. "What if someone comes in unannounced?"

"They'd better not," Dexter stated. "That's why I have a secretary. And Mrs. Langley announces herself before she comes in. Of course, it would still probably be best if you didn't make much noise while you're here. Unless, of course, everyone already knows you're here."

Dallas nodded. "I don't usually do much banging about as I audit accounts. Tends to distract me."

"If you say so. Ready to get started?"

"I suppose. Just show me how to get into the computer system and how it operates."

Dexter flipped on the computer and punched in his access code. "I think it would avoid a lot of hassle if you just use my code. That way, if any of the employees should notice it, they won't have any cause to wonder about it. They'll just think it's me.''

He showed her how to get into the accounting and reservation files. There were ample supplies of pencils, pens and pads of paper in the desk, along with other office supplies.

"If you need anything, just come and get me. If you need to make any calls, use line one. That's my line. Line two rings in here. So don't use that one to call out, or Mrs. Langley will see it light up on her desk and wonder why I'm using the phone in an empty office.''

Dallas hoped she was getting all of this. "I shouldn't have any problems and I shouldn't need to make any calls, but I'll just depress the button for your line now so that if I do pick it up, it'll already be on the right line.''

Dexter nodded and backed toward the door. "Dallas, the first moment you find anything fishy, you let me know.''

"I will," she said, turning her eyes to the computer screen and the most recent entries on the spread sheet.

Half an hour later Dexter quietly entered her office, his arms full of computer readouts. "These are hard copies of the accounts from the past six months. Let me know if you need to go back farther.''

The next four hours slipped by uneventfully as Dallas methodically went through the records of transactions, accounts payable and receivable, petty cash withdrawals and deposits and reservation deposits and payments.

She hadn't had much time to delve into each separate division, but Dallas was certain about one thing: there was definitely something out of balance with the Hotel Hudson's books.

The door opened and Dexter stuck his head in. "It's almost five-thirty. Ready to leave?''

Dallas nodded and made a few notations about where she was and what she was examining before shutting off the terminal and rising. She looked at Dexter and saw the question in his eyes. "You were right, Dex. There's something wrong with the books. And I don't think it was a mistake or sloppiness.''

"How can you tell?"

Walking into his office, Dallas rubbed her temple. "Because a mistake or bad bookkeeping would leap out at me. There's nothing so obvious here. It's very subtle. And, from the way it looks, whoever's responsible for it isn't taking huge amounts of money at a time. However, since it looks consistent, a thousand dollars or so every other month can add up after a while."

Dexter's mouth was set in a firm line. Dallas shivered and was glad she wasn't the one who was stealing money from him—or had stolen money from his grandfather.

"One other thing you should know, Dexter," Dallas said slowly. "I think that whoever's behind it has stopped. From what I've ascertained from going over the records of the past six months, I think the tampering stopped just after you took over. The latest entries are different from the older ones."

"So they just stole from my grandfather and not me? I wonder why."

Dallas smiled ruefully. "I couldn't imagine."

"Well, they'll find out they were right not to want to cross me. I don't care if they aren't stealing from me. In fact, to me, stealing from my grandfather is a worse offense."

Dallas couldn't help but think that old Mr. Hudson would have been proud of Dexter. Howard Hudson had cared about Dexter and about his happiness. He had loved his grandson, and Dallas now realized how little love Dexter must have known while he was growing up.

Dexter remained grim as they left the hotel and walked to her car. Dallas looked up at him after getting into the vehicle and starting the engine. "Dexter, I don't think it would be wise to dwell on this whole thing until I'm able to trace the source."

His expression softened a bit as he looked down at her. "Thanks, but I don't think that's possible. Especially now."

"Well, I think you should try. This could take weeks to finish, and you'll only give yourself an ulcer worrying about it all the time."

"Yes, Mother," he said contritely.

Dallas blushed and looked away. "I didn't mean to sound bossy."

Dexter leaned forward and rested his forearms on the door of the car. "I know. I was teasing you. I appreciate your concern, and I will try to put it out of my mind. Of course, it would help if I had something, or someone, else to think about."

"Why don't you think about ways to improve your mind?"

He laughed and stood up. "All right. I get it. Be careful driving home, and don't forget that lunch is at my house tomorrow at noon. Bring your suit and we'll go swimming."

Dallas waved at him. "I won't forget. See you tomorrow."

Later that night, after eating a light dinner and watching a few television programs she didn't remember the plots of, Dallas wandered restlessly around her apartment. Throckmorton followed her nervous movements with confused canine eyes.

Over to the window. Now to the kitchen. Open the refrigerator. Close the refrigerator. Over to the stereo system. Turn the radio on. Flip through the stations. Turn the radio off. Over to the sofa. Sit down. Stand up.

Into the bedroom. Take off her clothes. Put on her nightgown. Sit on the bed. Stand up. Over to the dresser. Fiddle with perfume bottles.

Throckmorton sat in the doorway, his big head moving back and forth as he watched Dallas pacing. He whined in sympathy, and Dallas whirled to face him.

"Oh, Morty, I'm sorry. Have I worried you? Come here, boy." As the big dog lumbered over to her, Dallas knelt down to scratch behind his ears and look at him eye to eye. "I'm all right, Mort, really, I am. I'm just thinking too much about you know who. Actually, you don't know who.

Dexter. Dexter Hudson. You'll meet him tomorrow. If he gives you a bad time, bite him. In a place where it doesn't show.''

She stood up, walked over to her closet and opened it, stooping to rummage around in the back among several boxes stacked there. Finding the one she sought, she backed out of the closet and sat down on her bed. Throckmorton jumped up on the bed, as well, causing a depression that threw Dallas off balance. The box she held in her hand tipped over and photographs and momentos spilled over the bed.

''Morty! You know you're not allowed on the bed. Get off.''

Morty yawned, got off the bed and lay on the floor so he could keep an eye on Dallas.

''You're just lucky you didn't ruin any of these, you bad dog.''

Morty yawned again and went to sleep.

''That's the trouble with all you Neanderthals,'' Dallas muttered. ''You just don't care. Live for the moment and for yourself.'' Gathering up the photos and replacing them in the box, Dallas sighed. ''Okay, so I'm being a little unfair. Stereotyping people isn't right. Dexter's an individual, and I should reserve judgment until I have the facts.''

It was then that her hand stilled. She was holding a snapshot of herself and Dexter and several other people at Lake Winnipesaukee. Kathy had taken the picture. Dallas, Kathy and several of their friends had gone up to the lake to go boating and waterskiing. Dexter had invited himself and Jill Karlen, Doreen's ex-best friend, to go along at the last minute.

Dallas studied the picture intently. Her hair had been very long then, and she'd braided it to keep it out of her face. Dexter had been standing next to her, with Jill plastered to his side. But he had been pulling on her braid with his free hand. Just as Kathy had snapped the picture, Dallas had looked up into his face....

* * *

Click.

"Got it!" Kathy yelled. "And all of you had your eyes closed."

Dallas tried to retrieve her braid as the group broke up, but Dexter wouldn't release it.

"Let go, Dexter," she said, her voice low.

"You've been avoiding me lately, haven't you, Waco? Why is that?"

Dallas glanced around, wondering if they were garnering unwanted attention. "I don't know what you're talking about, Dexter. Let go of my hair."

"Not until you tell me why you never come out to ride unless you know I'm not there. My grandfather told me you'd called and asked when I'd be there. Are you afraid of being alone with me again?"

Staring at his wide, naked chest, Dallas forced herself to shake her head and lie. "No, I'm not afraid to be alone with you. Why would I be? For that matter, how could I be? You seem to be trying to break a county record for how many different girls you can go out with in the least amount of time."

His gray eyes narrowed. "Jealous?"

"Hardly," she lied again, unaware of the vulnerability that was shimmering in her big green eyes. Seeing someone approaching from behind him, she stepped back. "I think you should leave me alone and remember the girl you brought with you."

"Here, Dex, put some lotion on my back. I can't reach it."

He turned his attention to Jill, and Dallas retreated to her own beach towel. Kathy was sitting on the next towel, and she hadn't missed anything. "What is it about big-breasted girls with no brains that attracts men?"

Dallas scowled. "My mom said that men who go out with women with great bodies and no brains are psychologically underdeveloped. That may be true, but I think Dexter is just after one thing from a girl. And it isn't a good conversation. I told him he was a Neanderthal, and he is. They operate on one level—physical instinct. Some men don't think with their brains. Dexter's one of them. And, not that you asked, so is Chris."

"He is not," Kathy protested, looking over at her boyfriend, who was preparing his sailboard to take it out. "We talk a lot."

"Uh-huh. What about?"

Kathy frowned. "I don't know. Things. What difference does it make?"

Dallas shrugged. "Never mind. It probably doesn't make any difference."

She lay down and settled her radio earphones over her ears, shutting out the world. She had no idea how much time had passed when she felt cold water dribbling on her stomach. Sucking in her breath, she jerked to a sitting position to find Dexter laughing at her. Pulling off the earphones, Dallas looked around and was dismayed to find that everyone had left. "Where is everyone?"

"They're waterskiing."

Her eyes cut quickly to the lake where she saw the motorboat full of teenagers pulling two behind it. Looking back at Dexter, she frowned. "Why aren't you with them?"

Shrugging, he settled himself on her towel. "Maybe I didn't want to leave you here all by yourself. They all thought you were asleep when you didn't answer them. And you're burning."

Dropping her eyes to her exposed stomach, Dallas could see that he was right. Reaching for her beach bag, she extracted her sunscreen and was about to put some on when Dexter grabbed the bottle.

"Hey, give that back."

"Nope. I'll put it on for you."

Dallas shook her head while she tried to swallow a sudden lump in her throat. "No, I don't think you should."

But he had already squeezed some lotion into his palm and was rubbing his hands together. "Maybe I shouldn't, but I'm going to. Move your hair."

Dallas reached back and pulled her braid over her shoulder. "Really, Dex, I don't think it would be a good idea—"

Her words died on her lips as his slick hands touched her warm skin. "Lie down."

She lay down on her stomach and let him spread the lotion over her back and legs, feeling every touch of his hands right in the pit of her stomach. She wanted to moan from the pleasure she felt, but she bit her lip.

"Turn over."

She heard the raspiness of his voice, but turned over, anyway, and gazed up at him through slitted eyes. He stared at her as he rubbed the lotion onto her legs and over her stomach, but when his hand touched her chest, she stopped him.

"Why are you doing this, Dex? Do you think it's fun to tease me and then laugh at me?"

Moving his hand from her chest to her waist, Dexter smiled sadly. "I don't know why I'm doing it. And I'm not teasing you, and I'm not laughing at you."

"Then why?" Tears gathered in her eyes, but she blinked them away.

"I don't know," he whispered, leaning over her and blocking out the sun.

Dallas knew she could have stopped him, could have run away. But she didn't want to. His lips were warm and persuasive and so much more skilled than those of the other boys she'd kissed.

Dexter's lips and tongue became more demanding, and Dallas was willing to give him all he asked for. Until his hand covered her breast. Her body jerked, so startled was she at the unexpected, although not unwanted caress.

Dexter pulled away and stared down at her, moving his hand away. "I'm sorry. I didn't mean to frighten you."

"You didn't," she whispered. "I was just surprised. Dexter, why are you doing this? You said I was too young, and you've been going out with all those other girls.... Why this? Why now?"

"Because I'm leaving tomorrow and I wanted to kiss you again before I left. I wanted to feel you."

He was leaving, she thought. And next summer she would be going away to college. She'd probably never see him again. "If you have to go," she managed to say, pushing him away and standing, "just go. Why did you have to make me—" She caught herself just before saying the words. She couldn't love him. He was leaving.

Stuffing her towel into her bag, she fought for her composure. "Why did you have to make me crazy the whole time you were here? Why couldn't you have picked on somebody else?"

One broad shoulder shrugged up at her. "Nobody else would've been so much fun . . . or responded so well."

Sighing distractedly, Dallas placed the picture in the box with the others and replaced the lid. "Oh, Morty, what am I going to do? I don't know what he wants or what he thinks about me now. Or why I care what he thinks. If he's only teasing me or leading me on... If he knows what's good for him, he'd better not be anything but absolutely sincere. I'm not falling for any he-man attitudes this time. This time—there is *no this time*."

After replacing the box in the closet and preparing for bed, Dallas crawled under the covers, still muttering warnings to herself not to fall for Dexter. But as soon as she closed her eyes it was his face she saw in her dreams.

Chapter Five

Dallas left her office at eleven the next morning and headed home to get Morty and to pack a duffel bag with her swimsuit, towel and cover-up, along with her hair dryer and makeup. She had intended to refuse Dexter's offer of pool privileges until the temperature climbed to eighty by ten o'clock that morning. She saw no logical reason to refuse his offer.

The top was down on her convertible as she sped along the highway, the wind in her hair. Morty, his ears flying behind him, had his head stuck around the windshield, the full force of the wind pelting his panting face.

"Isn't this great, Morty? The wind in my hair, the wind in your ears. You'll like it at Dexter's, Mort. Lots of grass and trees and shrubs. Dog paradise."

She pulled into the driveway and noticed that Dexter's car wasn't there. Glancing at her watch, she noted that she was a little early and figured he would be arriving soon. Morty didn't wait for an invitation to exit the car. He jumped onto the ground and made his way immediately toward a large elm tree.

Dallas climbed the front steps onto the porch and rang the doorbell, then whistled for Morty, who bounded up the steps and sat expectantly at her feet. Mrs. Foley opened the front door, and as Dallas smiled at her, she saw the woman staring openmouthed at Morty. Dallas tried not to laugh and kept her voice casual. "Didn't Dexter say I'd be bringing my dog?"

The woman gave Dallas a withering look. "Dog. Yes, he mentioned a dog. But that . . . are you sure he's not a Shetland pony?"

"Yes, I'm sure," Dallas laughed. "The vet said he's probably part mastiff and part Saint Bernard, but anything else is possible, too. He didn't say anything about him being part equine."

"I suppose he'll be expecting soup bones and the like?" Mrs. Foley frowned, but Dallas could tell she was secretly intrigued by Morty.

"Woof!"

The deep bark startled the housekeeper into laughter. "Smart, too, huh?"

Morty wagged his sizable tail.

"Well, come on in. Dexter just called a few minutes ago and said he would be a little late. He said you should go ahead and have a swim and that he'd join you for lunch as soon as he could."

Dallas nodded as she followed Mrs. Foley through the hall and into the kitchen. "I'll just let Morty outside and then change. He needs to stretch his legs, anyway." She opened the back door, and Morty loped out into the yard, bypassing the pool and heading straight for the meadow.

"You can use any of the rooms upstairs for changing," Mrs. Foley said.

Dallas nodded and started for the stairs. She chose one of the empty guest rooms to change in and left her duffel bag on the sheet-covered bed as she tied the sash on her cover-up and stepped into a pair of rubber thongs.

Mrs. Foley met her in the hallway before she could reach the stairs. "Oh, hello, Mrs. Foley. Is something wrong?"

"No. I was just on my way back up to the attic. I've been going through some of the things that old Mr. Hudson stored up there." The woman gave Dallas an intense stare. "There's some interesting old furniture and personal effects up there. Like books and pictures."

Dallas thought the woman was hinting at something, but didn't have any idea what it was. "Really? You know, the local historical preservation society might like to have anything Dexter would donate—anything he wasn't personally attached to, that is."

"I don't think he knows about most of that stuff. Like the pictures."

Dallas frowned. "Mrs. Foley, are you trying to tell me something?"

The older woman shrugged. "Maybe. I know you said you knew Dexter once several years ago. It wouldn't by any chance have been a summer when he spent some time here with his grandfather, would it?"

"Why, yes, it was. How did you know? Did Dexter tell you?"

"No. I recognized you from one of the pictures."

"Pictures?" Dallas was wondering why Mrs. Foley didn't just tell her what she was talking about, when the woman started walking down the hall toward the servants' stairs.

"Yes. The pictures in the attic. I thought I recognized the girl in some of them. It was you."

With that, Mrs. Foley disappeared up the stairs to the attic. Dallas, wondering why Mr. Hudson would have pictures of her in his attic, followed. Had *Dexter* actually saved pictures of her? If he had, he didn't remember them. Still, curiosity about the pictures compelled Dallas to climb the stairs and join Mrs. Foley in the musty attic.

"I raised the shades," Mrs. Foley said as she sat down on a piece of covered furniture. "But there isn't any other light. The bulb's burnt out. I tried to open a window to get a breeze, but they're stuck."

Dallas looked around the shadow-filled room. The small attic windows didn't allow enough of the bright sunlight in to illuminate all the corners.

Pieces of furniture covered with sheets took up most of the space in the attic. Dallas walked over to the windows and decided to try opening one of them. It was too hot and close to bear without some fresh air. After a few moments of struggling, she managed to get it open, and the fresh air that poured through was a welcome relief.

"Well, isn't that refreshing," Mrs. Foley intoned as she sat fanning herself with the lid from an old shoe box. Dallas nodded and turned back to the various shapes. The nearest one was most likely a chair, and she pulled gently at the sheet. It was indeed a chair, a wingback, probably as old as the house. Dallas ran her hand over the fabric. It was satin, and in wonderful condition.

"Mrs. Foley, have you looked at this furniture? It's beautiful. And it's probably worth a lot of money. Why is it stuck up here instead of being downstairs in the parlor or the living room?"

She went from piece to piece, pulling the sheets back carefully so as not to get any dust from them onto the furniture. There was a divan, a highboy, a desk and a cradle. All were in perfect condition.

"I don't know why they're up here. Old Mr. Hudson must have put them in storage along with these boxes." She gestured toward several cardboard boxes that were stacked beside the divan on which she sat. "I just got around to looking up here yesterday. It took me a month to get the first two floors cleaned and ready for decorating."

Dallas perched on the edge of the divan next to Mrs. Foley and peered at the photographs she held. They were mostly of Dexter in various candid shots, but then the housekeeper held up a picture that caught Dallas's eye. It was indeed herself in the picture with Dexter. They were holding croquet mallets in mock-threatening poses.

"Oh, I remember this," Dallas exclaimed. "Mr. Hudson had us set up the croquet set and challenged us to a game. I think it was Dexter and me against Mr. Hudson and Dexter's sister, who was up for the weekend.''

Mrs. Foley nodded. "Is Holly the one who took the picture?"

Dallas shook her head. "I don't remember. Actually, I think Dexter and I had just lost and Holly wanted a picture to prove to her friends that Dexter didn't win every game he played. Of course, he then tried to blame it all on me, and I told him to take it back or I'd whop him with my mallet."

Mrs. Foley chuckled, then showed Dallas another picture. It was a duplicate of the one Dallas had of them at the lake. "Yes. I have a copy of that one, too. It was taken up at the lake about a week after the other one was taken."

"Oh, my Lord," Mrs. Foley exclaimed, jumping to her feet. "I left the soup simmering. No, you stay and look at the pictures as long as you like. Then come down and have your swim."

With that she left, swinging the door shut behind her. Dallas smiled and looked back at the pictures. There was only one other picture of her in the pile. It was a picture she'd never seen. She didn't know who had taken it, but guessed it must have been Dexter or his grandfather. It was a picture of her and Freelance sailing over a jump. Tears stung her eyes at the memory of her beloved horse. She missed him more than she had thought.

Dallas laid the pictures on the divan and stood up. Sitting around looking at pictures of that summer wasn't what she'd had in mind when she came over. She wanted to go swimming. Dexter would be home soon for lunch, so she didn't have much time.

Walking over to the door, Dallas reached out and realized there was nothing to grasp. There was no doorknob or latch of any kind on this side of the door.

"Wonderful," Dallas moaned, and leaned against the door. "Now what do I do?"

Doubting Mrs. Foley would be able to hear her from the third floor, she didn't bother yelling. She considered climbing out onto the roof and yelling from there, but after seeing the steepness of the roof, she thought better of it. She'd just have to wait for Mrs. Foley to wonder where she was and come looking for her.

Sitting on the divan, she wondered absently how anyone could have gotten it through the narrow doorway. Then she sat up straighter. No one could have. Several of the pieces were too large to get through the doorway and would have been difficult getting up the stairs, too. There had to be another way.

Dallas looked at the shadowed walls and dismissed them. She got up and walked over to the window. Half way there she stepped on a wrinkle in the rug and looked down. Stepping down harder, she realized it wasn't a wrinkle. She dropped to her knees and felt the area. Hinges! It was a trapdoor. Of course. Using a block and tackle and a trapdoor would have been much easier than carrying the furniture up the stairs.

She knelt down, eagerly pulled the rug back and saw a two-sided trapdoor. Unlatching it, she pulled one side back with a little leverage and much protesting of long-unused hinges. Then, opening the door completely, she leaned over and peered into the gray hole created by its opening. "What the...?" Darkness. Well, actually, not complete darkness. She could make out hulking shadows below her. Thinking about the floor plan of the house, she surmised this was one of the empty guest rooms that was being used for storage. With the shades drawn and the door shut, very little light filtered into the room below her.

Leaning over, Dallas called out. "Mrs. Foley? Help! Can you hear me?"

Hearing nothing, she shrugged. Getting down shouldn't present too much of a problem. She swung her legs around so that they dangled through the hole, then gripped the handle on the other half of the trapdoor. Lowering herself through the opening, she hung there a moment, trying to decide if there was anything underneath her. Her thongs slipped from her feet. She heard a muffled thump and the louder sound of one thong hitting the wooden floor.

Something was definitely below her. Maybe it was a sofa. It couldn't be too far a drop, even with the high ceilings in the house. She and Kathy used to jump off Kathy's garage when they were kids, and this couldn't be any farther than that.

But there hadn't been any furniture underneath them then, either. And what if it was a table instead of a sofa? Or what if she landed on the back of a sofa? She peered down, trying to see if she could swing free of the object below, slightly to her left. One more try, she thought.

"Help! Mrs. Foley!"

She swung one leg out, and it hit a lamp or something that crashed to the floor. She winced. Now there was glass on the floor. And her feet were bare. And her arms were tiring. She heard footsteps and called out.

"Mrs. Foley, I'm in here!"

A door opened behind her and light from the hallway filtered in. Dallas's voice sounded relieved. "Mrs. Foley, I'm so glad you heard me. Could you push that sofa over so that I—"

The hands that closed around her waist weren't those of the housekeeper. The thrill that shot up her spine told her who it was. "Dexter! You're home."

His voice sounded amused. "It would appear so. And not a moment too soon from the look of things."

He lifted her and gently lowered her to the floor. When she turned to face him, she smiled sheepishly. He stepped aside so that she could leave the room, and then followed her into the hall. When she turned in the guest room to face him again, she noticed for the first time that she was practically naked. Her cover-up had come untied and hung open, revealing her bikini-clad body. She could tell by the look in Dexter's eyes that he had noticed.

"I can explain all this," she began. "You see, there's this attic room, and Mrs. Foley was showing me some pictures and some furniture and . . ." He was smiling that sexy smile at her again, and she forgot what she was saying. She couldn't think of anything but that damn smile and those damn eyes.

Dexter stood there for a moment as if he couldn't believe her. Then he ran a hand over his face and chuckled. The rich, deep sound washed over Dallas like a warm breeze, and she laughed, too.

Then his laughter stopped as his eyes roved over her body, and she felt a blush creeping up her neck and spreading over her cheeks. His eyes followed its progress, and when he finally looked into her eyes, his smile was a ghost. His eyes were smoky pools of desire and his voice was slightly husky. "Please don't ever lose the ability to look like that."

Dallas shook her head. "I'm not sure I know what you mean."

He stepped closer to her, and she had to tilt her head up to see his face. He reached out and touched her throat, sending tingles along the nerve endings throughout her body.

"Good," he said. "That means it isn't intentional."

His gaze drifted to where the front of the red bikini was joined by a piece of string. Dallas knew her breathing was causing more movement than normal. To her embarrassment her breasts swelled and her nipples hardened to erect points under his gaze, stretching the thin fabric of the bikini.

She took an involuntary step backward and felt the smooth polished wood of one of the posters of the bed pressing into her back. The bed? Oh-oh, a little voice warned, this wasn't right. She knew she was too vulnerable just now, but when she turned away to get more clothes to put on, Dexter leaned forward and placed his large hands on either side of her throat, caressing her throbbing pulse. He was so close that she could feel his warm breath on her lips.

"What is it about you that makes me want you so?" he asked.

Before she could even think about forming a reply, his lips were on hers in a searing kiss that melted her bones, and she sagged against him. His arms went around her and held her in a velvet vise, one at her waist, the other around her shoulders, his hand thrust into her hair.

His tongue teased the inside of her upper lip, and she opened her mouth eagerly. He plunged past her teeth and met her tongue. Dallas heard a groan and felt its reverberation, but she couldn't tell if it came from herself or from Dexter.

Finally, needing air, they pulled apart, but Dexter's lips were on her neck then. She gasped and felt her toes curl into the thick carpeting when he nibbled the sensitive spot beneath her ear. Her fingers were tangled in his thick dark hair, and she massaged the cords of muscle in his neck.

His lips traveled downward over her skin, and she arched toward his mouth without thinking. His questing hands pushed at the edges of the bikini top impatiently, and then one side fell away, exposing one creamy globe to his gaze. He lowered his head and covered the pink tip of the breast with his mouth.

Dallas gasped as desire shook her body, and she clutched Dexter's shoulders to keep from falling.

"God, you're exquisite," he murmured against her breast. The feel of his warm, moist breath filled Dallas with a need—the need to feel more of him. Just as she was pushing at the blazer he wore, she heard a noise from downstairs. Her eyes flew open and saw the door standing ajar. Mrs. Foley must still be downstairs. She was also flooded by embarrassment over how easily and how wantonly she had almost given herself to Dexter. How could she forget her own rules so easily? What was he doing to her?

Dexter sensed the new tenseness in her body and shifted his gray gaze from her breast to her wide green eyes. She tried to look away, but his eyes held hers in an invisible grip, and she could only stare back. His eyes held questions she wasn't ready to answer yet. They seemed so deep that she was afraid of falling into them and never returning. She shook her head slightly to clear her muddled thinking.

He smiled at the futile gesture. "It won't help."

Dallas still struggled for her composure. "Mrs. Foley is somewhere downstairs, you know. She could come looking for me. For us."

He nodded and pulled the strap of her swimsuit back into place with what Dallas thought was a reluctant sigh. That done, he took her hand and raised it to his lips. Then he stepped back and smiled. Dallas's emotions were torn. A part of her was disturbed at her lack of control, but another part of her was disappointed that Dexter was releasing her.

He reached out and traced the edges of the bikini top with a tanned forefinger. "I want you, Dallas," he said softly. "But I want you to be sure it's what you want. I think it is. But if this is too fast for you, tell me."

Dallas was unnerved by her own reactions, and Dexter's softly spoken concerns were too much to deal with right now. She couldn't let herself care that much for him. It wouldn't work. He didn't want the same things from her that she wanted from him. She let her eyes rove over his face, looking for some clue that he cared more for her than a brief fling.

Seeing the indecision in her eyes, he drew a deep breath and let it out slowly. "You're not sure."

Dallas dropped her gaze and stared at the top button of his open sport shirt. She wanted to tell him how she felt, but she was afraid. Afraid of leaving herself too vulnerable to the pain he was capable of inflicting.

She'd been hurt by Dexter once and never wanted to experience that kind of pain again. And she knew that if she gave in to her desires now, without knowing more about Dexter and what he was thinking and feeling, the pain she'd felt at seventeen would seem trivial in comparison.

Looking up into his eyes, Dallas saw the desire for her there, and she trembled slightly, fighting down her own desire to ignore her better judgment. But she couldn't. He must have seen her decision in her eyes, because Dallas saw a flicker of regret in his. "I'm sorry, Dexter. I'm not sure we should—"

He grasped her chin and forced it up when she looked away again. When her eyes met his, he smiled and kissed her lightly. "Don't worry about it. I understand."

She wasn't worried about anything except that she was falling in love with him. And she couldn't tell him that. So she nodded and hoped he didn't ask her to say anything, because she doubted she was capable of speech.

He stepped back and ran his hand through his dark hair. "Mrs. Foley is making lunch. Meet me downstairs?"

Dallas nodded again and he left. She sank down on the bed and stared at the ceiling. What was she going to do? If she continued seeing Dexter all the time, she would fall in love with him, and she still had reservations about their compatibility. As she pulled on her slacks and blouse, she wondered why it was that things in her life couldn't just be simple and uncomplicated. She was still muttering to herself about it when she walked downstairs to join Dexter.

As she entered the kitchen, she noticed that Mrs. Foley wasn't there. She paused in the doorway, wondering how she was going to be able to talk to Dexter after their rather steamy clinch of a few minutes ago. Then she heard a scratching at the kitchen door and started for it to let Morty in. Dexter must have heard the noise, too, because he was opening the door before even seeing Dallas.

He had barely gotten the door open more than a few inches when Morty shoved past him. As Dexter gaped at him, Throckmorton reared up in greeting. Dexter tried to get away from the huge dog and fell back against a chair, toppling over onto the floor.

Dallas raced to him to see if he was hurt, and found Morty sitting on Dexter's chest, trying to lick his face. "Dexter," she said, laughing, "are you all right?"

"Get him off me!" came the muffled reply.

Dallas grabbed the dog's collar and pulled him away. She scratched Morty behind his ears and shooed him back outside after giving him the soup bone. When she turned around, Dexter was standing at the sink, trying to wash away dog kisses. He picked up a hand towel and dried his face while Dallas hoisted herself onto the countertop next to him and let her feet dangle. Finally he put the towel down and faced her. "Why didn't you tell me you had a horse?"

"You never asked me how big my dog was, Dexter. Besides, you should feel honored."

"And why is that?"

"Throckmorton doesn't kiss just anybody. He must really like you."

Dexter placed his hands on the countertop on either side of her hips and leaned over to within inches of her face. "What about you, El Paso," he teased softly. "Do you kiss just anybody? Or do you only kiss people you really like?"

Dallas felt her stomach tighten and her breathing become erratic. She tried to sound flippant, but knew she was failing. Somehow it didn't matter. "Well," she told him, "there's kissing and there's *kissing.*"

One dark eyebrow rose as he considered her cryptic reply. Then he smiled. "Do you kiss anybody else the way you kiss me?"

Dallas had been staring at his lips. Now she raised her eyes and stared into his gray depths. She slowly shook her head. "I've never kissed anybody the way I kiss you." She raised her hand and let two fingers trace his lips. "No one has ever kissed me the way you do."

At the look of desire flaring in his eyes, Dallas knew she would fall under his spell again unless she did something. So she leaned over and kissed him on his warm, slightly rough cheek. He understood her unspoken message and, after swinging her off the counter, he asked her what Mrs. Foley had been talking about. "I walked in the door, and she said she'd found furniture for the parlor in the attic."

Dallas smiled her thanks for his understanding and sat in the chair he pulled out for her. They began talking about the house and the furniture, and Dallas felt grateful to Dexter for allowing her the chance to regain her emotional footing. She was afraid that it was becoming more and more difficult for her to concentrate on the fact that she wasn't completely confident of Dexter's trustworthiness, especially when he touched her.

The rest of the week flew by as Dallas gathered materials and waded through a paper trail that had to lead somewhere to someone. She'd gone back two years in the computer files without finding any clues to indicate who was doing the creative accounting.

And creative it was. Dallas had never seen anything like it. None of her courses had quite covered this type of embezzlement. So far all she knew was that every other month or so the profit and loss statements were different. They should have been consistent, but every six to eight weeks would show a drop in profit of between eight to fifteen hundred dollars. What Dallas couldn't figure out was why the books still seemed to come out right. She knew something was wrong; she just hadn't been able to pinpoint how they had done it.

Dexter was able to start eliminating members of the hotel staff who hadn't been working there two years previously. As Dallas continued to work backward, more people were crossed off Dexter's list of employees.

A few people had seen her entering the hotel with Dexter one afternoon, but they had only reacted with a smirk and a raised eyebrow. Dallas didn't doubt that the Concord gossip machine would make sure everybody knew they were an item by nightfall.

On Friday afternoon Dexter invited her to come over Sunday morning for breakfast and a relaxing day of picnicking, riding and swimming at his house.

"Oh, Dexter, I don't know if that's such a good idea."

"Why not? I think we both deserve a day completely devoid of numbers and suspects and sneaking in the back door."

Dallas knew she should say no. She needed time to be alone and try to figure out what was going on in her mind and in her heart. However, she wanted to spend the day with Dexter. Maybe they'd finally get a chance to have a serious, uninterrupted talk. Her feelings for him were growing, and she needed to know if he felt the same or if he was just looking for a few laughs and some good times.

So it was that Dallas was headed toward Dexter's house early Sunday morning. Morty, his ears flapping in the breeze, was happy to be asked along.

It was just after eight when she arrived to find the door to the kitchen unlocked. Dallas knew that even though she had the day off, Mrs. Foley was rarely gone for very long. Looking at the kitchen table, she noticed that the wild-flowers that regularly adorned the table were missing. Mrs. Foley must have thrown the latest bouquet away and not had time to replace them.

Dallas looked out the window at the meadow and made her decision. She was out the door in a flash, running toward the meadow. Throckmorton heard her and left his squirrel-watching vigil to join in the flower-picking frolic. After gathering an armload, Dallas headed back to the house, a contented smile on her lips. She found the vase under the sink and placed the flowers on the table. Breathing deeply of their scent one last time, she turned herself to the preparation of breakfast. She thought about going upstairs and waking Dexter, but felt it was probably wiser to let the frying bacon do the job.

She popped a cassette into the tape recorder she'd brought with her, turned the sound down and proceeded to gather the ingredients for blueberry pancakes. Rock music filled the room, the rhythm causing Dallas to grab a spatula and join the band.

She let Throckmorton in when he scratched, and he sat happily munching the bacon she threw to him while she sang. Morty was used to this. Dallas liked most kinds of music, so she listened to whatever matched her mood. Right now she felt like some good old-fashioned rock and roll.

As she swayed to "Rock and Roll Music," she set the table and went over to the refrigerator for the juice. She got out the pitcher and gyrated back to the table as the next song played. Then, stopping at the table, she put down the juice, grabbed her fork and starting singing again.

The sound of clapping stopped her private performance, and she whirled around to find Dexter leaning against the doorjamb, a smile of delight on his sleepy face. Her own face turned bright red and then she started laughing at the sight she must have made singing into her fork. She put the fork on the table and returned to the counter to mix the pancake batter.

Heavens, he looked sexy! He was wearing only the bottoms of a pair of pajamas, and they rode low on his narrow hips. His hair was tousled and he needed a shave. To Dallas he looked beautiful. When the music tape clicked off at the end of the song, Dallas looked up and smiled guiltily. "I'm sorry if I woke you. I didn't realize it was that loud."

Dexter pushed his large frame away from the doorway and went to the cabinet to get a glass. As he reached up, Dallas found that she couldn't help but stare in appreciation at the way his muscles moved in his back and arms. She quickly returned her gaze to a fascinating cupful of flour just as he turned. He sat down at the table and poured himself a glass of juice. After taking a sip of the cool liquid, he plopped his chin in his hand, rested his elbow on the table and looked at her.

"Actually, I woke up a little while ago. I could have sworn I saw a girl and her horse picking wildflowers in my meadow."

She laughed and spread her arms in the direction of the flowers. "My horse and I are guilty, but we won't repent."

"Are you always this chipper in the morning? Where did you hide the coffee?"

Dallas added two eggs to the batter and smiled at him. "Yes, I usually like the mornings, and I didn't hide the coffee. I just don't drink it. But I believe that Mrs. Foley left the automatic ready for you."

He strolled over and flipped the switch, and the coffee began dripping into the glass pot. Then, scratching his stubbled chin, he looked at her. "You don't drink coffee? Most people can't live without it."

Dallas nodded and drained her juice glass. "I know. My dad's like that. But I never liked the taste and so I never got hooked. If you never become addicted to caffeine, you don't need it to wake up."

He yawned, turned to get a coffee mug down and poured himself a cup when it was ready. After taking a sip, he joined her at the counter. "I didn't ask you here to cook for me, you know."

Dallas gave him a sidelong look. "Of course you did. You thought I'd show up and see that your idea of breakfast was a few stale doughnuts and coffee and then I'd feel compelled to make breakfast for you."

He grinned. "Looked in the cabinet, did you?"

"Yes, I found those hard old doughnuts. Mrs. Foley would kill you if she knew you'd put them there in a desperate ploy for attention."

Laughing, he headed for the door. "Just so I get a good breakfast, I don't care what I have to do. I'll go shower and change and be right back."

"I don't believe I'm doing this," she said to herself aloud. Morty gave a small woof, and she looked at him with a frown as she stirred and poured the batter. "I'm laughing and joking with him. Cooking him breakfast. What's the matter with me?" Afraid that she already knew the answer to that question, she refused to dwell on it further and got on with the pancake making.

Ten minutes later she heard whistling, and Dexter strode into the room. She tried to ignore him and concentrated on pouring more batter onto the griddle. Why did he have to be so sexy? It wasn't anything he did, exactly. It was just the air of masculinity he exuded.

The physical attraction she had thought would die had only grown. She was finding that she actually liked Dexter, something she'd never expected to be possible. The whole situation was making her nervous. Now, as she watched

Dexter walk into the room, she was overwhelmed by an unaccustomed anxiety. Would he like her cooking?

She immediately derided herself. What possible difference could it make and why should she worry? She was a liberated, intelligent woman. She wasn't really domestic. So why was she suddenly worried about whether or not this giant would like her pancakes? Irritated by her own inner turmoil, she didn't see the expression of appreciation on Dexter's face.

"This looks great," he said as he sat down and reached for his fork. Dallas watched his biceps move and ripple into the chest muscles that strained against the fabric of his shirt. He was casually dressed in jeans and a short-sleeved gray polo shirt. His dark hair was still damp from his shower, and it curled against his forehead.

When she didn't respond to his words, he waved his hand in front of her face to snap her back into the here and now. She jumped and then shook her head to clear her thoughts. Smiling, he leaned toward her. "I don't know where you were, but can I go with you sometime?"

Dallas laughed. "Sure, but I rarely go to the same place twice."

"Good. I like variety." He paused and then stabbed a sausage. "As I was saying, this looks great. Did Foley tell you blueberry pancakes were my favorite?"

No, Dallas thought. *You did. Six years ago at the diner off the highway where we stopped for breakfast before driving out to the lake. I remember all sorts of stupid little things about you. I tried to forget, but I couldn't.*

Dallas tried to shrug noncommittally, but when he praised her cooking, she couldn't help smiling with pride. She berated herself again for her archaic attitude, but she couldn't stop the positive feelings flooding through her. She took her own plate of warming pancakes to the table and sat down, thinking that most people who went insane were committed to mental institutions. Dallas Shelby was apparently fated to be insane in her own way. Crazy in love with Dexter Hudson.

Chapter Six

After they washed their breakfast dishes, they went for a ride through the meadow and onto a path through the woods that bordered it. Dexter owned twenty acres of land, and Dallas thought they must have traversed every one of them.

Not having ridden for more than a month made the outing feel like a special treat for Dallas. She thought she saw Dexter smiling indulgently at her and asked him what he was grinning about.

"I was just remembering how fierce you were when I teased you about your horse. You would have thought he was Secretariat or something. I guess I still can't believe you sold him voluntarily."

Dallas felt a pang of remorse as she thought about her horse. "It was one of the hardest things I've ever done," she said softly. "But, in a way, it was almost like I'd expected it. My mother was gone and my father was barely there. Then..." *Then you came and left,* she thought.

"Then what?"

"Um . . . then, after I won the blue ribbon in that horse show the fall of my senior year, I was accepted at Princeton. My trainer asked me what I planned to do with Freelance. I had no idea what he meant. I asked my father for his opinion, but he was busy and just said it would be all right to leave Freelance where he was and that I could ride him whenever I came home. But I knew that wasn't going to be very often, so I told Ted to find some good people—people who would love him and ride him often—and I sold him."

Dexter sat on his horse, watching the emotions playing across her face. "Would you do the same thing if you had the chance to do it again?"

Dallas nodded. "Yes, I would. I was sad, but it was the best thing for Freelance." She looked over at Dexter and tilted her head quizzically. "Didn't you ever have a pet you had to give up or that died? Most people have to deal with that sort of thing when they're young."

"No, I never had a pet. My mother said they were too messy. I learned to ride at boarding school, but I never had a horse of my own until my grandfather bought me one. My sister got one, too. He kept them here, and we'd ride when we came for visits, but it wasn't like having one all the time. Holly's made up for her lack of childhood pets, though. She's always taking in strays now. I've just been too busy the past few years to bother with having to care for an animal."

Dallas thought that was too bad. Morty was a great support to her sometimes. He was more than a pet; he was a friend.

Mrs. Foley had returned from church by the time they put the horses away, and was packing them a picnic lunch. When they invited her to join them, she declined by shaking her head.

Dallas and Dexter took their time walking across the meadow to the edge of the large copse of trees they'd ridden through earlier. Throckmorton was thrilled to be included and barked happily when Dallas waved his rubber football at him. It was his favorite toy, and he always took great care not to clamp his powerful jaws over it too tightly. He had destroyed two Frisbees that way. Dexter placed the picnic basket on a blanket under the shade of a huge elm tree, then sat down to watch Dallas play with her dog.

"Okay, Morty," she said in a huddle with the big dog. "I want you to go out ten and cut left. On two. Got it?"

After an excited "woof" and a vigorous wag of his over-size tail, Dallas patted Morty on the head, and he ran over to sit about ten feet from her. She then leaned over the football, grasped it and spread her legs. Dexter sat beneath the tree, watching everything with a big grin.

"Twenty-nine!" Dallas yelled. Throckmorton crouched, getting ready to run on her signal. "Sixty-three!" she yelled, and the big dog seemed to tense all over, not even moving his tail. "Hut! Hut!"

Throckmorton bolted from his crouch, sending divots of grass flying in his wake. The dog ran straight and then suddenly broke to the left as Dallas sent the rubber football spiraling toward him. He leaped into the air and caught it, then continued running until he got to within a few yards of Dexter and the tree, where he sat down and dropped the football at Dexter's feet.

"Touchdown!" Dallas screamed, jumping into the air. Throckmorton panted an imitation of a smile and wagged his tail enthusiastically. "The crowd goes wild! Once again the combination of Shelby and Guildersleeve has proven unstoppable!"

Dexter laughed and Throckmorton barked happily.

"Unstoppable against whom?" Dexter asked as he picked up the slightly soggy football.

"Why, the entire New York Jets defensive backfield," Dallas explained. "Throckmorton's just too fast for them."

Dexter rose swiftly and gracefully and tossed the football into the air and caught it. Dallas frowned slightly. Dexter was planning something. He was eyeing Dallas critically as she watched him in her baggy short-sleeved sweatshirt and faded jeans.

"So you like football, huh?"

"Sure do. Morty and I watch the games every Sunday during the season."

Dexter juggled the ball thoughtfully, then threw it to her without warning. She was surprised, but her reflexes were good and she caught it. Dexter inclined his dark head slightly and said, "Not bad. But how do you fare against competition?"

Dallas knew what he was driving at and shook her head. "Oh, no. If you think I'm going to play football against a Neanderthal like you, you're crazy. I value my life."

Dexter walked slowly toward her, his usual smile in place. "Now, Dallas," he coaxed, "you know I'd never hurt you."

As she stared into his eyes, she knew he had meant her to understand the double meaning. But she didn't want to get into that particular discussion yet.

"Maybe not," she conceded. "Intentionally, that is, but I'd have to be certifiable to go up against a former collegiate bone crusher like you."

When he just stood there, grinning, she poked a finger into his hard chest. "You thought I'd forgotten, didn't you? Dexter Hudson—Yale's defensive captain. Captain of the so-called 'quarterback attack squad.' And now you want me to pit my pitiful 115 pounds against the brute who led the 'quarterback attack'? No way!"

Dexter was still laughing at her editorializing when he reached out, grabbed her upper arms and lifted her straight into the air. The football dropped onto the ground as her fingers lost coordination. He pulled her up to his eye level, and she could feel the controlled power in him. He wasn't hurting her, but the sheer strength of the man made her gasp in awe.

"Ivy Leaguers aren't allowed to be brutal," he said. "A future doctor's hands might get hurt."

"Right."

"We always played ethically and mannerly."

"Uh-huh."

"Are you going to let me play?"

"Hey, bruiser, no problem." She grinned. "It's your yard."

Dexter kissed her swiftly and set her down. "That's right." He bent down, picked up the football and handed it to her. "So, do you want offense or defense?"

Dallas put her hands on her hips, the rubber ball propped under one hand, and looked up at him saucily. "As if it makes any difference." Then she smiled. "Offense. Morty and me against you."

Dexter's head swung around to look at the big dog. "I don't know... two against one..."

Dallas snapped her fingers, and Throckmorton trotted over and plopped himself at her feet. "Maybe so, but since our combined weights probably don't add up to yours, it's fair. Besides," she added, "it's Morty's football."

"All right," Dexter agreed.

They took up their positions opposite each other. In the rules of touch football as they played it, Dexter couldn't move for five seconds after the ball was snapped. If he touched whoever had the ball, it was downed.

Dallas gave Morty the same instructions as before. Actually, it didn't matter what she said, because he always did the same thing. He was strictly a one-play dog. But Dallas had a strategy of her own in mind.

"Twenty-seven!" she yelled, knowing that was Dexter's age. She looked over at her dog and crouched. "Twenty-eight next month! Hut! Hut!" she yelled as she saw the surprised look on Dexter's face.

Morty took off downfield. By the time Dexter saw where Throckmorton was, Dallas had thrown the football. The dog jumped up and caught it, then loped toward the tree where the picnic basket was. Sitting down he released the ball and wagged his tail.

"Touchdown!" Dallas shouted.

"Well, I'll be damned."

Dallas pranced about for a minute and then ran over to Throckmorton and hugged him. Then she grabbed the football and waved it in the air. "Shelby and Guildersleeve slip past the quarterback attack for six points! The crowd is stunned!''

Dexter pointed a finger at her. ''I didn't know you were the kind of girl who plays dirty.''

Dallas eyed him slyly. ''What kind of girl did you think I was? One who would let brute strength win out over strategy?''

He laughed, and the sound filled the meadow and Dallas's heart. ''I suppose I must have underestimated you. But it won't happen again, Dallas. You can count on that.''

She knew he meant more than the literal words, but didn't say anything. Walking back to where he stood, she handed him the football. ''Your ball,'' she told him. Then, turning back to where Throckmorton sat, she signalled him to come, pointed at Dexter and said, ''Listen, boy, he's got your ball, and we've gotta get it back. Are you with me? Good!''

The next half hour was a series of stunts that might have been more at home on a blooper show than a football field. Dexter never had a chance when Dallas and her sidekick had the ball, but when he had it, he used his own strange strategy, which sometimes worked and sometimes didn't. Once, he sneaked past Throckmorton by throwing a stick in the other direction. Dallas cried penalty, but to no avail. The next time he tried it, Morty caught the stick in midair and reared up on Dexter before he could score.

''That'll teach you to be sneaky,'' Dallas crowed.

She and Morty were winning by twelve points and they had the ball. But when Dallas pulled back to throw the ball, her dog spotted a rabbit and took off to chase it, leaving Dallas three seconds before Dexter could move.

''Oh-oh,'' was all she could manage as the big man straightened and looked to see where her errant wide receiver had gone. When he turned back to face her, she laughed nervously. ''Now, Dexter,'' she began as he advanced. ''Time out! Dexter?''

''Don't you mean, 'Neanderthal,' Dallas?'' he teased.

She grinned and continued to back away sideways, hoping to surprise him and make a fast break. ''Oh, now, Dex,'' she said sweetly, "you know I was only kidding. I have a great deal of respect for your...um...physical attributes."

When she saw the flare in his eyes, she thought she might have a chance. She put the football behind her back, stretching the material of the sweatshirt across her full breasts. Just as she hoped, his eyes moved down in appreciation of her body, and she broke to the right and was almost home free when his fingers grasped the edge of her shirt. He reeled her back slowly and caught her around the waist with one arm and took the football from her with the other.

"Interception," he said softly, pulling her against him.

As his mouth descended, Dallas felt her body respond eagerly. His lips moved over hers firmly and aggressively. Dallas wrapped her arms around his neck and pulled herself even closer to him. Her mouth opened to receive his tongue, and she met it with her own.

She heard what sounded like a growl from Dexter, which made her tremble. It was the sound of desire. Her mind couldn't keep up with all the sensations her body was experiencing, but one thought registered loud and clear: *she wanted Dexter Hudson.*

She heard another sound. It was barking. Morty. Oh, not now.

But the barking was then followed by the screaming of a woman.

Dallas's eyes flew open, and she stared at Dexter for a split second before they were both running. Dallas took the time to straighten her clothes and hair before following Dexter across the meadow toward the house.

When she rounded the copse of trees that separated the back lawn from the part of the meadow where they had been, she saw Dexter running toward the swimming pool. She heard him call Morty's name, and the dog stopped barking as Dallas reached them.

There was a woman standing on the ladder of the high diving board, looking absolutely terrified. Dexter was laughing at the poor woman. "Oh, come on down, you big baby. He won't hurt you."

"Dexter, I've just had a horrible brush with death, and if you don't make that dog go away, I'll never speak to you again!"

Dallas watched the strange exchange with wide eyes. Who was this woman? She looked up at the woman, who had turned pleading eyes to her. Dallas blinked in surprise. It was Holly. Dexter's sister.

"I don't know who you are," the woman said, "but could you please make the dog go away?"

Dexter laughed again. "No, wait until I run and get my camera. This sight has to be preserved on film."

Dallas reached up and touched Dexter's forearm. "Don't be mean, Dex."

He turned laughing eyes to her and said, "It's my job to be mean to her. She's my sister."

Dallas smiled up at the woman. "I know that. But, nevertheless, you didn't think it was very funny the first time you saw Morty, either."

She reached down and shoved the dog. "Go on, boy. Go back to the house."

Morty barked happily and ran off in the direction of the back door. The woman then descended the ladder. "Thank you. It's nice to know someone still has a heart."

"You're welcome. I'm sorry about Morty, but he really wouldn't have hurt you."

Dexter laughed again. "Not much. The animal knocked me down."

Holly smiled over at Dallas, then frowned. "Don't I... Oh, my gosh, I do know you, don't I?"

Dallas smiled. "Sort of. We met about six years ago, here."

"Yeah, don't you remember Lubbock Shelby?"

"Dexter, if you don't stop that inane—"

"Oh, sure," Holly interrupted. "Dallas Shelby. Your dad's the congressman from this district, right?"

Dallas nodded. "Yes, he is. He was then, too. Sometimes I think he always has been."

As they walked toward the house, Dexter casually looped his arm over Dallas's shoulders, and she glanced over at Holly, whose eyes had widened slightly.

"Well, I'm glad to meet you again, Dallas. Very glad."

Dallas continued to smile across Dexter at the tall brunette walking on his other side. "It's mutual. No doubt Mrs. Foley was glad to see you."

"No doubt," Dexter snorted.

Laughing, Holly patted his arm. "Now, now, don't be bitter. I didn't mean to interrupt your fun with your—"

"Accountant. Dallas is auditing the hotel books for me."

Dallas felt a pang of disappointment at Dexter's words but remained silent. Holly simply raised her dark brows in disbelief. "Sure," she said. "Do Mother and Dad know about Dallas being your...accountant?"

She emphasized the words to make sure Dexter knew he hadn't put anything over on her. Dexter just smiled. The arrogant oaf. Dallas extricated herself from his arm and opened the door to the kitchen.

"No, they don't," he said as they sat down at the table. "And I don't want them snooping around. They'll find out soon enough."

Holly turned her gaze to Dallas. "Sorry to talk about you in front of your back, but old habits don't die in our family. But now..." She looked at her brother. "Well, it would seem that Mother might smile upon her only son again."

"I beg your pardon?" Dallas felt as if she'd come in on the second act of a play. Dexter frowned at his sister, and Holly seemed vasty amused about something.

"It's nothing," Dexter finally said. "Holly's just being facetious." He turned his gaze back to his sister. "What brings you up here, anyway? Isn't New York holding your interest anymore?"

Holly smiled, then waggled her finger at him. "No, it isn't that. I just decided to come up and visit my big brother and spend a relaxing few days in New England. And I brought some papers for you to sign that finally make the Long Island Hudson Hotel mine. Mine. Isn't that a lovely word?''

Dexter grinned. ''Lovely. Yours. Your hotel, your staff, your budget problems, your chef problems, your delivery—''

''Yeah, yeah, I get your drift. What a wet blanket. But, anyway, that isn't the only reason I came up. I wanted to tell you something.''

''What, your phone doesn't work?''

Holly shook her head. ''I've been overworked for the past couple of days, and I needed to get away, anyway. Besides, some news should be delivered in person.''

Dexter glanced at Dallas, then back at his sister. ''Well?''

Holly didn't say anything at first, but dropped her hand in front of her to toy with the wildflowers. Dallas noticed the ring on her finger immediately, but Dexter, apparently, wasn't quite so attuned. Still, he saw a look exchanged between the two women. ''All right, what is it?''

Dallas laughed. ''Don't be dense, Dexter.'' Her eyes darted purposefully at Holly's hand. Dexter's gaze followed hers and his eyes suddenly widened in comprehension.

''Oh, look, Dallas,'' Holly exclaimed, pointing to a spot over Dexter's head, ''a light bulb!''

''Cut it out,'' Dexter warned. ''So when did this happen? Who is this guy?''

''His name is Jeff Bryant, and he's a perfectly wonderful man. And if you say anything to him that's the least bit derogatory, I'll never speak to you again.''

Dexter grinned. ''I guess you must be in love. And I wouldn't dream of picking on your intended. Where is he? Hiding in the dining room?''

''No, he isn't,'' Holly sniffed. ''He's in New York. He couldn't get away for another few weeks.''

''How long are you planning to stay? And when are you and your intended intending to pledge your troths or whatever?''

"Careful, big brother," Holly warned sweetly. "Or I might start to ask embarrassing questions."

"Stay as long as you like, anytime. What do you want for a wedding present?"

Holly suddenly rose and threw her arms out in an expansive gesture. "I nearly forgot my second most special reason for coming to see you, brother o' mine."

Dexter looked at her warily. "And what would that be?"

Holly held up an index finger. "I'll be right back," she said, running through the swinging door.

Dexter sighed. "I don't like this. Holly's surprises are never normal."

Dallas laughed. "I like her."

"I'm sure you do. It's two against one."

The swinging door opened and Holly entered, one hand held behind her back. "Close your eyes."

"No way. You've probably got a banana cream pie back there."

Holly crooked her finger at Dallas. "Look behind my back, Dallas, and inform this wimp that I don't have a pie in my hand."

Dallas dutifully rose and looked behind Holly's back. She laughed. "No, Dex, it is most certainly not a banana cream pie. Close your eyes."

Grumbling again about everyone ganging up on him, Dexter nevertheless closed his eyes. After a moment, Holly announced that he could open them.

Sitting in Holly's outstretched hands, about two inches from his face, was a tiny calico kitten. Dexter blinked and pulled his head back. "It's a cat."

"And we wondered why he graduated magna cum laude from Yale," his sister teased.

"Isn't it cute, Dexter?" Dallas didn't know why Holly had brought her hulk of a brother a kitten, but it was absolutely adorable.

"Well, yeah, I guess so. Thanks, Holly. I think."

"My landlady's cat had kittens, and I promised to find a home for this one," Holly explained. "I thought about you all alone up here in New Hampshire, but that was before I knew about you and Dallas. And Dallas's dog. Maybe it wasn't such a good idea.''

Dallas thought that Dexter was going to correct his sister about the state of their relationship, but he didn't. Instead, he took the kitten from her and held it gingerly. ''Oh, I don't think Morty will hurt it. Do you, Dallas?''

She smiled. ''No, I don't think so. But it might be a good idea if we introduced them and let them get to know each other slowly.''

Dexter nodded and patted the kitten's head with his huge finger. The kitten purred and Dexter laughed. ''Is this a girl cat or a boy cat?''

Holly chuckled. ''Can't you tell by the way you've got her purring and snuggling?''

Dallas nodded but didn't say anything. Holly was right. Women were probably always purring for Dexter Hudson. She knew she did.

Mrs. Foley, who had been unashamedly, albeit quietly, eavesdropping from the utility room, came into the breakfast nook and shook her head. ''If that doesn't beat all I've ever seen,'' she said, looking at Dexter holding the kitten.

''Foley, darling,'' Dexter said, ''I thought you had Sundays off.''

''I do, and I'm just now on my way to a bridge game at Hannah Carlyle's. I don't like to butt in, but if you young folks wouldn't mind a suggestion?'' When they shook their heads, she pointed through the window toward the meadow. ''If I were you, I'd go get that picnic lunch that's been sitting out there. If that horse-dog gets a whiff of ham sandwiches, there won't be any food left.''

With a startled ''Oh!'' Dallas was up and running, Holly on her heels, laughing and trying to get assurances that Morty wouldn't really bite. Dexter remained seated, laughing at them and stroking the tiny kitten's fur.

They managed to get to the food before Morty. Her dog had had other things on his mind, Dallas was sure. Because if he'd wanted to destroy the picnic basket and all its contents, it wouldn't have been much of a chore for him.

She and Holly took it back to the house where they ate the food with Dexter, who then roped them both into finding a bed and litter box for his new pet.

"Peripeteia?"

Dallas stared at the Scrabble board. Dexter, having used all seven of his letters adding onto an existing word, had just leaped ahead by about two hundred points. He now leaned back and nodded. Lady Macbeth, the newly named feline, sat on his shoulder, peering down at them. "Sure. Peripeteia. You know, reversal of the situation and recognition scenes...from Aristotle's *Poetics.*"

Holly smacked herself on the forehead. "Of course! My goodness, Dallas, how could we have been so dense?"

Laughing, Dallas covered her face with her hands. "I don't know. I feel so inadequate now."

"What?" Dexter asked with a straight face.

Holly shoved her chair back and rose. "Since my brother has effectively put my winning this game out of the realm of possibility, I'm going to bed."

Dallas looked at her watch. "But it's only nine-thirty."

"I want to take a nice long bath, then I think I'll read for a while." She glowered mockingly at Dexter. "Maybe it'll improve my vocabulary."

Holly left, taking Lady Macbeth with her, and Dallas smiled ruefully at the board, mainly populated by Dexter's long, ancient words. "I think she's right. I'd probably have to go back to school and study for another four years just to be able to challenge you at this game."

"Oh, I don't know," he offered. "You're pretty good."

"Pretty good wasn't good enough to keep from being creamed by you. Where did you learn all that stuff?" Her hand indicated the playing board.

Dexter's eyes twinkled with humor. "I may have majored in business, but I minored in literature."

Dallas sighed. "Naturally. The next thing I know you'll be quoting John Donne."

Leaning forward and capturing her hand, Dexter kissed her palm. "Do you like Donne?"

Her voice barely qualified as a whisper. "Yes."

"Then I'll reacquaint myself with him for you," he murmured, his thumb stroking her pulse.

Dallas tugged to regain her hand. "I don't think that would be such a good idea, Dexter."

"Why?"

"I don't think we know each other well enough for you to be reciting Donne's poetry to me."

Dexter paused, assessing her expression. "Does he do that much for you?"

Frowning at the spot on her wrist where he'd been rubbing, Dallas didn't think before she said, "It's not just him, but you and him together. I don't think I'm ready for that."

"Ah," he said, as if he understood.

Dallas realized what she'd said and gritted her teeth. "My mouth—"

"Is luscious," Dexter said as he lowered his lips to kiss her gently.

The tension in her jaw relaxed and the rest of her body followed, and she found herself drawn into Dexter's lap. When she felt his hand smoothing along the skin of her back, she tensed and pulled away. "I should be going, Dex."

"No, you shouldn't," he denied. "But it's probably better that you do."

On that cryptic note Dallas gathered up her purse and her dog and headed home.

The phone rang as Dallas was slipping her nightshirt over her head an hour later. The thought that it might be Dexter flitted through her mind, and she hesitated a moment, not sure what to say if it was him.

"Hello?" Her voice sounded small and tentative.

"Dallas? Is that you?"

Kathy! Dallas sighed and flopped down on her bed. "Hi, Kathy. Sure it's me."

"You sounded funny."

Twirling the telephone cord around her finger, Dallas agreed with her. "I feel funny."

"Aha," Kathy said knowingly. "Funny strange, or funny ha-ha?"

Dallas smiled faintly. She didn't want to think about why, but she'd been feeling especially lonely since leaving Dexter's house . . . or, more specifically, his arms. "I'll tell you all about it later."

Her friend's voice remained bright. "All right. I'll hold you to that. Now, as to what I called about. I've found John Hallett. He's from Manchester. I've got his office number and even his home number. Got a pencil?"

Dallas chewed her lower lip for a moment before replying slowly, "I don't think I want it, Kathy."

"What? Why not? I thought you wanted to corner him and make him fork over his half of the money?"

Dallas sighed. "I did. But I've changed my mind. I'd rather not ever see or talk to John Hallett again. I'm already doing Dexter's audit as repayment for the mirror, and he said that even though it won't cost as much and even if we didn't find John, he'd still call it even. So what's the point of it?"

Kathy sniffed. "The principle of it, for one thing."

"I know, Kath. But really, I'd rather not have anything to do with John . . . ever." A pause ensued, and Dallas knew Kathy was considering asking her about Dexter. "I'll tell you later, Kath. I don't think there's enough time left before dawn to do it now."

"Just so you know I'm always here, pal."

"I know. And I appreciate it. Really."

"Okay, well, I'll let you go now, but I'll call you tomorrow at work and we'll set a time to go out to lunch or dinner or something."

"Sounds good."

After hanging up, Dallas lay back on her bed and contemplated the ceiling. Her feelings about Dexter were confusing and so sensitive that she couldn't even talk to Kathy about them yet.

It had been a disturbing day all around. She'd expected Dexter to affect her senses but hadn't expected such a rapid capitulation of her heart. It was just that Dexter was so hard to resist. She was beginning to wonder why she was resisting at all. Maybe it was time she opened her mind a little to who Dexter was now, instead of who he may have once been . . . or seemed to have been.

Chapter Seven

During the next week, Dallas meticulously sifted through more of the computer records of the hotel. She could have progressed more quickly if she'd been able to keep her mind totally on the job and off Dexter. But that was next to impossible when she saw him practically every day for lunch and sometimes for dinner. And he was constantly in and out of her office, bringing her files, food and sodas.

On Thursday he just walked into her office and sat down. Dallas glanced up to find him watching her. "What? Did you want something?"

Dexter nodded. "Yes, I do. But I didn't think you'd give in so easily."

Futilely fighting a blush, she shook her head. "Very funny, Dexter."

"I'm serious, but since you're in a business mood, how about an update?"

Dallas sighed and leaned back in her chair. "I'm not positive, but I think I've pinpointed the method, if not the person responsible."

Her statement brought Dexter out of his chair. "Why didn't you tell me?"

"Dexter, I have to have more than a hunch before I go around pointing arbitrary fingers. For the past few hours I've been comparing some of the records I've already looked at with those from a few years back. I think the money's being taken by someone in reservations. Or at least someone with access to the reservations computer and till."

"Are you sure?"

"Well," Dallas replied, shrugging one shoulder, "from all indications, someone collected money from people staying in the hotel, then recorded the reservation as canceled and kept the money—except for the cancelation fee. Since that was still paid, no one questioned it. Also, since the housekeeping staff and the reservations staff don't interact on a regular basis, I doubt that these discrepancies were reported very often."

Dexter paced the room for over a minute, then stopped. "I have two managers, two assistant managers, an accounts manager and ten reservation clerks. How do we determine who the guilty party is?"

Leaning forward and placing her elbows on the desk, Dallas kept her eyes on Dexter's restless form. "First, we need your list of employees. We can then make up a new list from it after we eliminate those people who have been working here less than eight years. That's how far back I've gone so far."

Dexter disappeared through the door into his office and was back in less than a minute. He stepped around the desk and placed the list of hotel employees on the desk where they could both see it. Leaning over her shoulder, he peered at the list. "The list is in alphabetical order, with the employees' departments and starting dates in these two columns."

Dallas picked up a pad of paper and a pen and they began a list. Five minutes later Dallas put the pen down. "Not quite as long as we thought, is it?"

There were five names on the list. The two managers, the manager of accounts and two clerks. Dexter rubbed his neck wearily. "I don't know what to think from this. The day manager, Linda Marshall, and the night manager, Carl Anderman, have been working for this hotel for the longest amount of time. Linda for thirteen years and Carl for fourteen. Ken Wasserman's been the accounts manager for eleven years, and the two clerks are women who work part-time and are volunteers in community service. They've been here nine and ten years."

Dallas tapped her pen on the list of names. "I think our best course is to continue to go back and see if we can eliminate any more names from the list."

"I suppose so," Dexter agreed reluctantly. "But it's already almost five, and I have a meeting with some convention site committee members. Why don't you just go ahead and leave now and I'll—"

"Don't be silly, Dexter. I'll go ahead and finish up this quarter I'm working on, and then I'll leave."

Dexter frowned and shook his head. "I don't think that's a good idea. Someone could see you leaving and wonder why you're here without me."

"I suppose that's possible, Dex, but not really probable. People have seen me coming and going with you for two weeks and not said anything. Or have they?"

Shrugging noncommittally, Dexter sat on the edge of the desk. "If they're talking about us, it isn't to me. But, then, I didn't expect they would."

"Dexter," Dallas said firmly, "you go to your meeting. I'll leave on my own and I'll be very careful. I'm quite capable of taking care of myself, you know."

"Yes, I know. I'll go, but I don't want you staying past five-thirty."

"You're going to be late for your meeting."

"I'm going," he said, backing toward the door. "But if I come back here after my meeting and find you still here, I'll—"

"What will you do, Dexter? Fire me?"

He paused with his hand on the doorknob. "Obviously not. I have something else in mind for you."

"What," she asked suspiciously. "Torture?"

"Maybe. But an exquisite torture."

With that last remark he was gone. Dallas was still staring at the door a full minute later, her cheeks a bright red and her lips hinting at a smile.

It wasn't Dallas's intention to stay later than five-thirty, but she became engrossed in the records and time slipped past quickly until the lack of light in the room caused her to look distractedly toward the window.

"Oh-oh," she whispered, quickly glancing at her watch. It was six forty-five. Dexter must still be in his meeting.

Hurriedly shutting off the computer and gathering her purse and car keys, Dallas walked through Dexter's office and opened the door to his private entrance. She didn't see anyone and slipped outside, walking along the path to the hedge that bordered the parking lot.

Just as she stepped around the hedge and onto the sidewalk of the street that ran parallel to the hotel, where her car was parked, Dallas thought she heard footsteps. Halting abruptly, she listened, but didn't hear anything.

Her heart pounding and her legs shaking, she hurried to her car and jumped into it, locking her doors and then looking all around her. The sun had just begun to set, but there was still plenty of light to see if someone was following her.

Not seeing anyone, Dallas took a deep breath and let it out slowly. "It was just my imagination. Dexter's making me paranoid."

Starting her car and putting it into gear, Dallas decided not to tell Dexter about it. After all, no one was there and nothing had happened.

Pulling into her driveway ten minutes later, Dallas hurried into her duplex and was greeted by an enthusiastic Throckmorton. She checked her answering machine and was glad to see that no one had called. All she needed was for Dexter to have an attack of machismo, wondering where she was.

"All right, Morty, calm down. I'll feed you, I promise."

She went into the kitchen and pulled out Morty's food, mixing one large can of dog food with three cups of dry dog food. She hadn't managed to put it on the floor before Morty was gulping it down. "You pig. I should send you to obedience school for a course on manners."

The phone rang and she picked up the kitchen extension. "Hello?"

"Hi."

Just the sound of Dexter's voice over the telephone made her pulse jump.

"I just got home and thought I'd call to make sure you were all right and to get a progress report."

"I'm fine and I managed to get through another two years' of files, to the end of the computer files. That's ten years back. The irregularities are still there, so I guess that clears the two clerks. Tomorrow we'll have to start picking through the old ledgers and reservation cards. Do you even keep those things that long? Or, rather, did your grandfather?"

"I don't think so." Dexter's voice sounded tense.

"Dex? Is something wrong?"

"I think it's a pretty amazing feat to get through two years' of records in thirty minutes."

Dallas closed her eyes. When would she learn to think first and speak second? "Dex, I didn't mean to stay late, but I truly didn't notice the time. And when I did, I left."

"Don't you realize I set down those time rules for your protection?" he asked tartly. "What if someone had noticed you were in the system? It could ruin everything."

"I think you're being an alarmist. And I said it wasn't intentional. Besides, now that we have the list narrowed to three people—"

"Now that we have the list narrowed to three people, I can turn this whole matter over to a private investigator. I don't want you involved in this anymore."

Dallas gaped at the telephone receiver. "You can't be serious! I've put in so much time on this, and I'm so close to finding the source, Dexter. Don't get paranoid on me now."

"It isn't a case of paranoia, Dallas," Dexter said determinedly. "And I don't want to discuss this over the phone anymore. I'll be over in a few minutes."

"No, Dexter, there's nothing to— Hello? Hello?" She slammed the receiver onto its hook. "Paranoid Neanderthal," she muttered. "I ought to leave right now. Just get into my car and drive around Concord for a few hours. Let him pound on my door until his big, hairy knuckles bleed. That's what I ought to do."

Morty wagged his tail and whined at her. "Thanks for the vote of confidence, Mort. You're right, you know. If I left, I wouldn't have the pleasure of telling him what a jerk I think he's being."

"Woof!"

"You're right about that, too. Why should I care that he's pulling me off the audit? I didn't want to do it in the first place."

Morty went to the kitchen door and scratched at it. Dallas let him out. She then went into her bedroom and pulled off her work clothes, throwing them onto the bed, or the floor, or wherever else they happened to land. Jerking a sweater over her head and pulling on a pair of comfortable jeans, she was still muttering about Dexter when she heard his car roar up her driveway. Running to the front door, she put the chain on and waited. Thinking he would ring the bell, she was startled when he pounded on the door.

"Dallas! Open the door!"

"Who is it?" she called out from spite.

"Just open the damn door."

Unlocking the door, she pulled it open as far as the chain would allow and looked out at his tense features. "What do you want?"

"Unchain the door or I'll rip it from the wall."

The quiet words almost made Dallas back down. But she knew he wouldn't really do it. At least she hoped he wouldn't. "You do and you pay for it."

"I can afford it."

"Oh, all right."

She closed the door and slipped the chain off, then jumped back as Dexter practically slammed it open again. "Don't you ever try to lock me out again, or I swear I'll rip the whole door off its hinges."

"Is that a threat, Dexter? What are you threatening me with? You've effectively fired me from a job I was never hired for and now you're threatening to tear my door down. This is *my* house, and in here I'm the one who has the say-so."

Dexter walked past her into the living room, running a hand through his already tousled hair. "Dallas, it isn't that I don't think you're competent or that you're not good at what you do. You are good, obviously, since we're now so close to finding out who's been ripping off the hotel. It just makes more sense to call in professional investigators now."

"I don't see where it makes more sense to spend all that money to bring in strangers when another week or two of my going through the records will turn up the proof of who did it."

Dexter sighed. "Can you guarantee that?"

Taken aback, Dallas blinked at him. "Well, no, not absolutely. But there's bound to be—"

"In other words, you may find some positive proof and you may not. That's not good enough anymore, Dallas. Tell me, how much money do you estimate has been taken?"

"I don't know for sure. It's been taken at random, not systematically. But, roughly, so far, I'd say between seventy-five and eighty-five thousand."

He stared at her. "How could anyone get away with stealing that much money for so long? You said it's been going on for more than ten years. Why didn't it get spotted during tax seasons, or by another employee? Or during a general audit?"

"Because of the nature of the embezzlement. On the records it's put down as canceled reservations. Unless someone was looking for something wrong, like me, they wouldn't question it. Technically the books balance, but I saw the regularities of the canceled reservations. They should have been irregular. And the real ones were. It was the faked ones every six weeks or so that I began to question. That's when I saw the pattern start to emerge. Approximately every six weeks there's a week to ten days of unusually high cancelations. Then it returns to normal. The amount of money taken depends on what prices the rooms were."

"And the other employees wouldn't necessarily have noticed anything was amiss because the cancelation fees were there. Very clever."

Dallas almost blew a sigh of relief. "Yes. And in another week or so I'm sure I'll have traced—"

"No, you won't. As of right now, you're not involved in this anymore. And don't worry about the mirror. Consider it paid in full."

"I can't believe this. What do you think can happen? No one even knows I'm doing the audit."

Dexter reached out, grasped her upper arms and pulled her close to him. "I can't take the risk that they might find out before we catch them. I can't take the risk of your getting hurt."

Dallas was encouraged by the fact that Dexter was worried about her, but frustrated at the thought of being left out of the most interesting part of the whole plan. "I appreciate your concern, Dexter, but I can take care of myself."

His harsh laugh caught her by surprise. "You did a real good job of handling Hallett, didn't you?"

Dallas placed her hands on Dexter's chest and pushed, twisting out of his grasp. "Actually, I did. He wanted something from me I wasn't willing to give—and he didn't get it." Dallas couldn't contain the frustration she was feeling. It was as if he was taking an Agatha Christie novel away from her just as she began the last chapter. And she was powerless to stop him. "I think you should leave, Dexter. Since I'm fired and no longer have an obligation to you, there's no reason for you to be here."

He stared at her and laughed. "Don't be ridiculous. This is for your own good and you know it. And I have every reason to be here since I think it should be pretty clear by now that we belong together."

Her eyes widened in shock. "What's that supposed to mean?"

"What does belonging together usually mean? A man, a woman, spending a lot of time together. In this case, us."

Dallas stared at him, certain one of them had lost his or her mind. "I think I missed something here. Exactly what are you suggesting?"

"I'm suggesting that we stop playing games. We're good together." He held up his hand and pointed to his fingers one at a time. "We're young, intelligent, educated and from the same social background. We both like sports and we dislike politics. We're financially stable and have solid careers that we like and that are flexible."

"Well, how romantic of you. I don't recall you asking for my opinion."

His eyes twinkled down at her. "You give me your opinion every time I kiss you."

Bounding up from the sofa, Dallas poked him in the chest. "You really are a thickheaded, pea-brained—"

"It's an important factor and quite high on my list of priorities. Argue all you want, but you can't deny that we are and always have been sexually attracted to each other. Without that we'd probably just be friends, but with it... well, a more serious relationship is inevitable." He clapped his hands and rubbed them as if he'd just concluded a satisfactory business deal. "Well, it's been a fun evening, Austin, but I have to get going. I'll call you tomorrow."

He started for the door, and Dallas followed him to try to wedge in her two cents' worth of rebuttal. But Dexter suddenly wheeled around and pulled her into his arms, kissing away what few senses she possessed. Dallas, caught unaware, responded naturally before she could think.

Setting her away from him, he smiled down at her. "See? I'll call you tomorrow." Then he was gone.

Dallas stared at the closed door until she heard the car roar away. Then she slowly walked back into the living room and sat down.

"I'll get you for this, Dexter Hudson. Messing with my head and my heart. Turning my life upside down. Getting me all involved in an embezzlement case and then kicking me out. And now you think I'll be your significant other? Your footsie friend? You must be crazy. Ordering me around like some harem girl. You think just because you're a great kisser and have a great body and like my dog that I'll go along with everything you want? Hah! If I didn't love you so much, I'd hate your guts."

Confused by Dexter's strange proposition and feeling left out of the investigation, Dallas did something that even she couldn't explain. She went home. Assuming her father was out of town, as he usually was, Dallas wandered into her childhood home the next morning, not sure why she was there or what she wanted.

"Dallas!" Marie, the housekeeper, exclaimed when she saw Dallas walk in the back door into the kitchen. "What a surprise. How have you been lately? I heard you were getting serious with that Hudson boy. Or is that just a rumor?"

Staring with wonder at Marie, Dallas couldn't help but smile. "How do you do it? You always know what's happening in this town practically before it happens."

"Housekeeper grapevine," Marie confessed. "So it's true? You and Dexter Hudson?"

Dallas smiled wanly. "Right now, Marie, I'm not sure how true it is. I'm too confused to be sure about anything."

Marie leaned closer and peered into Dallas's eyes. "You're sure. You're in love."

Dallas sighed. "So I am. But is he? And can my love hold him if he doesn't love me? I have real doubts about that one, Marie. Loving a person doesn't guarantee they'll return that love, nor does it guarantee they won't leave you."

Sympathetic arms enfolded her briefly, then Marie sniffed and stepped back. "Times like this you need your mother most."

Dallas nodded and blinked away her tears. "I know. Maybe that's why I came by today. I think I needed to talk to her."

"Well, you go on into the study. If you need anything, just let me know."

Making her way into her father's study, Dallas sat down in a huge, overstuffed leather chair and pulled her feet up under her. Hanging over the fireplace directly in front of her was a portrait of her mother, painted the year her parents had married. Long, wavy chestnut hair framed a delicately beautiful face. Serene green eyes, so much like her own, gazed out at Dallas.

"Oh, Mama," Dallas whispered, "why did you have to go so soon? I needed you so much . . . and I still do."

Hearing the doorknob turning, Dallas looked up, expecting to see Marie.

"Dallas? What are you doing here?"

"Daddy? I didn't know you were home. I was just . . ." Dallas glanced away from her father's face and looked up at the portrait.

Her father followed her gaze. "I thought I was the only one who sat in here and talked with her."

Surprised green eyes collided with troubled blue ones. "Do you, Daddy? I had no idea."

Sighing quietly, Mr. Shelby made his way over to the matching leather chair next to Dallas's and sat down. "I guess I haven't shared much with you since your mother . . . passed away, have I?"

Dallas, surprised by her father's words, felt her throat constrict. She wanted to talk with him but hardly knew how. Yet she knew she had to. "I knew you were busy, Daddy.

You have a lot of responsibilities and obligations. You always did. I tried to be understanding after Mom died, but I never got the chance. I always felt as if you didn't really want to see me. Sometimes I felt you looked through me instead of at me. Marie tried to tell me that you were missing Mom and that I should be patient. But I missed her, too, and instead of having you to lean on, it was as if you'd left me when she did.''

Tasting a salty teardrop on her lips, Dallas hurriedly brushed her fingers over her cheek and took a deep breath. Her father didn't notice, and she thought, yet again, that maybe he'd understand her better if he'd just look at her—really look at her—once in a while.

About to tell him so, her words stayed on her tongue when she heard him clear his throat noisily. Was he going to get as emotional as his daughter? Dallas hadn't thought it possible.

Finally the congressman nodded. ''I suppose that, in a way, I did. Leave you, I mean, when she died. I should have...well, hindsight can't change anything. I'm sorry about everything you went through. A part of me wanted to reach out to you, but at the time I couldn't bear it. And then you went away to school and the time just got away.''

''What do you mean, you couldn't bear it?''

A sad smile touched his lips as he gazed up at the image of his late wife. ''I loved your mother very much, Dallas. And I was always proud of you. But when I lost her, it was too hard—you looked too much like her. Every time I saw you I saw her. I hadn't realized it until then, but you even sound like her. I avoided you because it hurt so much to see her in your face, to hear her in your voice.''

''Oh, Daddy,'' Dallas broke in, understanding finally dawning. She swallowed a lump in her throat and looked at him. His gaze didn't waver. ''I wish I'd known that then. Maybe I wouldn't have felt so...I don't know...so abandoned.''

''I know. It was wrong of me to shut you out. I'll regret it for the rest of my life. But maybe we can begin anew. I want to be here for you, Dallas. I do love you. I always have, even though I may not have shown it."

Dallas's smile was watery. "I think I always knew that, Daddy. I couldn't not believe it."

He then reached over and grasped her hands, pulling her into an awkward hug, but Dallas didn't care. It was a start. They would become close again.

Releasing her, Mr. Shelby sat back and cleared his throat again. "Now what's all that nonsense Marie's been babbling about lately? Something about you and Howard Hudson's grandson."

Dallas sniffled loudly but managed to laugh. "Never underestimate Marie, Daddy. And it's funny you should mention trouble and Dexter Hudson in the same breath...."

She then explained the bare bones of her situation with Dexter, leaving out much of the personal information, since she still didn't feel entirely comfortable talking with her father. Even so, just being able to talk with him at all was a step forward, and when Dallas left the house later, she felt more optimistic about the future of her relationship with her father than she did about her relationship with Dexter.

By the next morning Dallas had decided to avoid Dexter and to ignore his aberrant proposal until she could come to grips with her own turbulent emotions, but her determination ran into trouble when Cheryl buzzed her.

"There's a Mrs. Foley on the line. She wouldn't say why she's calling."

Dallas was surprised and wondered if Dexter had told his housekeeper anything. She thanked Cheryl and depressed the blinking button on her phone.

"Mrs. Foley? How are you?"

"Oh, I'm fine, I suppose. I was just calling to ask if you'd mind coming over here and supervising some workmen. My sister just called and needs me to take her to the doctor, and the workmen are already on their way over to take that furniture down from the attic and put it in the parlor."

Dallas frowned in puzzlement. "Don't you think it would be better if you got someone else? I mean, I don't really even work for Dexter any—"

"Oh, I don't think any of that matters, Miss Shelby."

"Dallas."

"Miss Dallas. Dexter's at work, and this wouldn't really put you out too much, would it? I suppose I could call a taxi for my sister...."

Dallas hurriedly agreed to help. "That's all right, Mrs. Foley. I'll do it. You go ahead and leave now. I'll be there in a few minutes."

It took two workmen three hours to get the furniture from the attic down into the parlor. Dallas felt as though her legs were about to give out as she climbed the stairs for what seemed the hundredth time. One of the temporary workers waved to her from the door of the guest room where the trapdoor stood open, a block and tackle hanging from a hook in the attic ceiling.

"Say, do you want us to leave the cradle up here, or what?"

"No," Dallas said, rubbing her weak thighs. "Put it in the nursery over there." She pointed. She wasn't sure what Dexter was going to do with it, but it just didn't seem right to leave the cradle all alone in an empty attic.

"Okay, that leaves the little couch."

"Divan," Dallas corrected, but he didn't hear her.

After watching the men struggling down the stairs with the deceptively heavy divan, Dallas didn't know how she'd muster the strength to walk back down the stairs. Just the thought of all those stairs, downhill or not, made her legs want to give out. Her gaze fell on the polished banister. Looking surreptitiously down into the empty foyer, she grinned.

Easing her leg over the rail to straddle the banister, she balanced herself by placing her hands lightly on either side of the gleaming wood and let gravity do its work. Her exhilarating slide to the foyer was over in just a few seconds.

She just managed to slow herself as she slid over the smooth curl of wood that marked the end of the banister.

"Where's a camera when you need one?"

Dallas gasped and whirled around, none too steadily, to face a grinning Dexter, standing in the doorway of his office and holding a file.

"What are you doing here?" she finally managed when she stopped gaping.

"I could say I live here, but I know that's not really what you meant." He held up the manila file folder. "I forgot a file for a project I'm working on and had to return for it. If I'd known you were having so much fun, I might have shown up before this."

"I refuse to be embarrassed by this," Dallas said defiantly, struggling to keep a serious expression on her face. "Mrs. Foley had to take her sister to the doctor and, out of the goodness of my heart, I came over to help her. My poor legs are very nearly worn out from climbing those stairs so often this afternoon. I was merely saving myself from certain collapse."

Dexter tilted his head to assess her jean-clad legs. "Of course, I could judge them better without the jeans, but if memory serves, your legs deserve any and all efforts to preserve them."

Despite her efforts, the blush Dallas had been fighting crept up over her cheeks at the thought of Dexter looking at and appreciating her legs. He grinned and took a few steps toward her. Leaning down, he kissed her reddened cheek. "Ah, there it is. I love it when you blush."

Dallas blinked up at him and stepped back, her back against the banister, and cleared her throat. "Why don't you stop making fun of me and go back to work?"

He laughed. "Oh, sure, run me out of my own house. By the way, I saw the furniture in the parlor. Looks like sissy furniture to me."

"Dexter Hudson, it's wonderful furniture. They're antiques and worth a lot of money. And they fit the parlor perfectly."

"Yeah, yeah," he said. "But can a man feel comfortable sitting on it?"

She rolled her eyes. "Don't worry. Mrs. Foley told me the living room will be filled with recliners and stain-proof carpeting so that when Yale loses to Princeton this fall and you spill your beer, it won't be hard to clean."

"Ha! Lose? No way. Yale's going to whip Princeton up one side and down the other."

Dallas nodded. "Uh-huh. Whatever you say."

"Ten bucks."

"I beg your pardon?"

He pointed at her in challenge. "I bet you ten bucks that Yale beats Princeton this year."

Dallas was about to remind him that the game wouldn't take place for another four months, but didn't. "All right, you're on. But I'm not cleaning the beer off the carpet."

"We'll see." He smirked and headed toward the front door. "I have to get back. Thanks for coming by. I appreciate it."

Dallas stared. He was sincere. How could she be grouchy when Dexter acted like a gentleman? "You're welcome. Um, did you hire your private investigator?"

Dexter nodded. "Yes, he's coming over to the hotel in about an hour. I know you don't like being left out, Dallas, but I think it's best."

"I know you do. I don't happen to agree, but it's your decision."

His gaze narrowed. "Yes, it is. But I do find it interesting that you aren't arguing about it anymore."

One shoulder rose and fell. "What good would it do? You won't be reasonable about it, so why should I—"

"Oh, I get it. You don't get your way, so I'm being stubborn and unreasonable. Is that it?"

"That just about covers it."

He pointed his file folder at her. "You know, you're no slouch in the stubbornness department yourself."

"High praise from a master."

"Are you going to continue to act like this and spoil our blissful future?"

"And that's another thing. I wish you would stop saying things like that. You're just doing it to goad me, and I don't think it's at all nice."

"Nice?" Dark eyebrows arched over gray ones. "Why would I want to be nice? That's pretty bland, don't you think? Besides, nice guys finish last, or haven't you heard?"

"And obnoxious guys don't finish at all."

Dexter opened his mouth, but the ringing of the telephone cut him off. He snatched the receiver from the phone on the foyer table.

"Hello? What? When? I'll be right there."

Dallas had watched the rapid changes of expressions on Dexter's face and knew he'd received bad news. "What is it?"

"There's been a fire at the hotel."

Dallas grabbed her purse from the table and followed Dexter out the front door. "What happened?"

"I don't know. But it was apparently localized."

Trotting along beside him as he headed for his car, Dallas hesitated, afraid that she already knew the answer to her question before she asked it. "Was it the office?"

"More specifically, your office." Stopping by his car, he turned to look at her. "I want you to go home and stay there until I check this out and talk with the private investigator."

"But, Dexter, I—"

"Just do as I ask, Dallas. Please?"

She nodded worriedly and turned toward her car. Then, watching Dexter roar out of the driveway, she wondered what was going to happen next. If the fire in her office had been deliberately set, then someone knew about the audit. How much further would they go to keep from being found out?

Chapter Eight

"I don't know what to think anymore, Kathy," Dallas moaned an hour later. She hadn't been able to endure sitting and waiting alone, so she'd called her friend, who had left work early to keep Dallas company.

They had ordered pizza and were waiting to hear from Dexter, who had been gone for two hours. Dallas had managed to tell Kathy practically everything she knew and most of her speculations in that time.

"This whole thing has got me so turned around that I feel like I'm lost in a house of mirrors. Should I just butt out? Is it really any of my business? If I don't, will I cause more trouble? What am I doing? And more importantly, why?"

Kathy pulled a piece of pizza loose, twirled the cheese around her finger and regarded Dallas. "The why is easy. You're in love. People do weird things when they're in love."

"Kathy, I don't know how it happened. I swear, I was still calling him a Neanderthal, and it sort of crept up on me."

Her friend smiled understandingly. "I know. It's like that sometimes. You just didn't recognize the signs because you've never been in love before. And I can't really say that I'm all that surprised."

"What do you mean? *I'm* surprised."

Popping a stray mushroom into her mouth, Kathy nodded. "I know. But you haven't been watching and listening to you for the past few weeks. I think I know more about Dexter Hudson than his mother does."

Dallas averted her eyes guiltily. "I guess I've talked about him a lot, huh?"

Kathy laughed. "Just a bit. But it was to be expected, the way you were thrown together. Especially with an attraction already present. You were just asking for trouble. Or love. Whichever way you want to look at it."

"But, Kathy, I don't think I want to be in love with Dexter," Dallas whispered.

"Sorry, Dallas, but there's not much to be done. As you know, I'm a firm believer in fate. I'm also a believer in food being the universal cure."

"So getting fat will solve all my problems?"

They looked at the ruins of the pizza that sat on the kitchen table. Her friend smiled and shrugged. "No, but it makes for more durable suffering."

Dallas laughed. "Right. What's for dessert?"

"Aha, I came prepared." Reaching into a tote bag she'd brought with her, Kathy removed a plastic container and pulled the top off with a flourish.

Dallas peered into it and sighed. "Chocolate chip cookies. Boy, you can always tell your real friends by how they treat you when you're down."

"Yeah," Kathy agreed, biting into a cookie. "They sacrifice their figures for you. But if you feel better, it's all worth it."

Dallas chewed on her cookie and smiled. "I do feel better, Kathy. Just having someone to talk to is a help. Worrying about the audit and whoever's behind it is bad enough, but Dexter's weird statements about us having a future together just make me more confused. Why would he say something like that?"

"Have you considered the fact that he might be serious?"

Dallas shook her head. "No. He's never said he loves me or anything. We barely know each other. I mean, a few weeks is hardly enough time to get to know someone."

Kathy nodded. "So you don't think you know Dexter?"

"No. I do. At least I thought I did. He's not as much of a caveman as he used to be. And that's something else I don't understand. I fell in love with him, anyway, knowing how overbearing and bossy he can be. How could I do that?"

"Maybe because you know there's more to him than that, and you love him despite his faults. And, not that you asked, but you can't judge love by the amount of time you've known someone. Knowing a person for years doesn't guarantee you'll love him, and lots of people swear they fell in love the first time they met. Different people react to love differently. Some look for it. Some try to avoid it."

Smiling shakily, Dallas cleared her throat. "I guess we don't have to figure out which category I fall into, do we?" She chewed another bite of cookie thoughtfully. "I want him to be serious, Kathy. I want him to love me, but I'm afraid that he doesn't."

"No, you're not. What you're afraid of is that he doesn't look at life the same way you do."

"What does that mean?"

Kathy considered her next cookie. "Dallas, there are a lot of things people can overcome in relationships. But one thing that can't be overcome is a difference in values, because they're the very basis of who we are and how we look at the world and the people around us."

Dallas nodded thoughtfully. "And when your values are different, it affects everything else in your life."

Kathy nodded. "Yes. And you, Dallas, for all your liberal politics, are a very conservative person. You've led your life by a strict set of private rules. You need a man who believes in those same basic tenets."

"I don't know. You're making me sound like some sort of paragon, and I'm not."

"No, you're not. That isn't what I meant. It's just that you can't compromise your personal values without feeling guilty. No one can. What's worrying you is that you're afraid Dexter doesn't share your values."

Dallas toyed with another cookie. "I know. I didn't think he did, but lately I don't know what to think about him. He's different, more mature, naturally, but something even more than that. I actually found myself liking him. Having fun with him. But he's never said how he feels about me, and I don't think I could continue a relationship unless he loved me the way I love him."

"Have you told Dexter you love him?"

Dallas shifted uncomfortably. "Well, no. What if he laughs? What if he says the whole thing was just a joke? I don't think I could stand it."

Kathy picked at a chocolate chip. "You know, maybe he feels the same way. Maybe he's afraid to open up to you. Maybe he's afraid of being rejected by you."

"That's ridiculous."

"Is it? Maybe you should think about it. Women aren't the only ones who are subject to the pain love can cause."

"I know, Kathy. It's just that . . . I don't know. I haven't done real well in the personal relationship department. Everyone I've loved . . . maybe it would be better if I didn't love him."

Kathy shook her head. "Wait a minute. I think I've just picked up on something I've been incredibly dense about for a long time. You think everyone you ever loved has left you?"

"Maybe not left," Dallas shrugged. "My mother was taken, I guess, and I didn't have to sell Freelance. And my dad didn't physically leave, although it felt like that at the time."

"And Dexter left you that summer," Kathy sighed. "I remember thinking that you were blowing the whole thing out of proportion that summer after he left. But you really did love him then, didn't you?''

"Yes, I did," Dallas admitted. "And he left, anyway."

"Did you tell him then that you loved him?"

"Of course not," Dallas said. "I knew he was only going to be there for a short time."

"But now he's back, Dallas," Kathy reminded her. "And you've had a nice talk with your father, and you might not have Freelance, but you have Morty. And your mother didn't leave of her own free will. As you said, she was taken—but your memories of her weren't. Maybe now you should be concentrating on your future and what you want out of life. And if you want Dexter, maybe you should get up the nerve to ask him exactly how he feels and what he wants. Because one thing you can be sure of—if you don't see this thing through and you lose him again, you'll always wonder about it."

Dallas thought about what Kathy had said and wondered if maybe she was right. Why should she expect Dexter to give her more than she was willing to give? She decided she would tell Dexter that she loved him and risk getting hurt, but the sound of his car pulling into her driveway weakened her resolve.

She pulled the door open just as Dexter was walking up the front walk. He looked up at her and smiled wearily. "Hi."

"Hi, yourself. You've been gone two and a half hours. How bad was it?"

Following him into her living room, Dallas gestured for him to sit down on the sofa and then sat next to him.

"It wasn't bad in terms of damage to the hotel, but all the hard copy files we were using in the investigation were destroyed, as well as the office itself."

Dallas nodded. "Did the firemen or police say what caused it?"

"It was definitely arson. A simple case of gas-soaked rags tossed onto the desk with the files and ignited."

"Did anyone see anything?"

He shook his head. "Nothing. I talked with every employee who was working at the time. No one saw anything unusual. My secretary was out of the office for lunch and a couple of other times on errands, so it had to have been set during one of those times—probably the last errand. I talked with the private investigator, and he's looking into the personal lives of the three people we suspect. But right now that's all we have to go on."

Dallas noted the lines of strain around his eyes and mouth and doubted he'd thought of food or rest at all. "You haven't eaten, have you?"

Dexter shook his head. "No. I'm not really hungry."

"Nevertheless, you should eat something. Kathy came over earlier and we ate a pizza. Lucky for you, it was one of those 'buy one, get one free' deals and there's an entire pizza sitting in my kitchen waiting for you."

He smiled softly at her. "Well, since you went to all that trouble...but unfortunately I'm a mess."

Dallas looked down at his hands and realized they were covered with soot. There were also streaks of black on his arms and clothes. "So you are. Well, go on into the bathroom and wash up while I heat up the pizza. Then we'll relax and watch a movie or something on TV."

He nodded and ambled into the bathroom while Dallas heated the pizza and poured them both a soft drink. Carrying the food into the living room, she placed it on the coffee table just as Dexter returned.

"I'm really not very hungry," he insisted again as he sat down.

Dallas just handed him a plate. Fifteen minutes later the pizza box was empty. "I'm so glad you weren't really hungry," she said wryly as she gathered up the dishes and empty box. "Because if you were, I'd be left with bare cupboards." She headed for the kitchen.

He yawned over a smile. "I guess you were right. I probably should be getting home."

From the kitchen Dallas called, "Are you sure you wouldn't like to stay and watch TV for a while? It might take your mind off the hotel and everything."

She didn't hear his reply, and quickly cleaned up the dishes. Turning off the light in the kitchen, she stepped out into the living room and smiled.

The television was on, but Dexter was sound asleep on the sofa, his head lolling to one side. Dallas walked over, picked up his feet and put them on the sofa. Then she placed her arms around his torso to slide his body into a more comfortable position.

"Mmm...Dallas."

Her heart fluttered. He was thinking of her in his sleep. That had to be a positive sign. And he looked so vulnerable asleep. Dallas slipped his shoes off and put a throw pillow under his head. Her index finger smoothed the lines of worry that were still present near his mouth. He sighed and she pulled her hand away.

She heard Morty scratching at the back door and went to let him in. "Now you have to be quiet, Mort. Dexter's tired and needs to sleep."

Throckmorton yawned at her and went to lie down beside the armchair that matched the sofa. Dallas sat in the chair and turned off the television. She picked up a magazine but couldn't concentrate on it. It was much more satisfying just watching Dexter sleep.

She was still watching him when he awoke two hours later. His eyes blinked open and he looked at her. Dallas didn't say anything.

"What time is it?" he asked.

She glanced at the digital clock on the VCR. "It's a little before nine. Do you feel better?"

He yawned, stretched and sat up, rubbing his neck. "I guess so. Sorry about going to sleep on you. I guess I was more tired than I thought."

"That's all right. You weren't exactly any trouble. Dexter, I have to tell you something—"

Dexter rose and held out his hand, then leaned over to put on his shoes. "Uh, do you think it could wait, Dallas? I'm beat and I really should be getting home. Tomorrow I have to get to work and figure out who's behind this. Uh, is he a good watchdog?"

Dallas looked down at Throckmorton, who was asleep. "Of course he is. Why?"

"Because I don't like the idea of leaving you alone and unprotected. Whoever set the fire knows there was an audit going on, so they probably know you were doing it."

She nodded. "Maybe. Do you think that whoever it is would actually harm me? I mean, trying to destroy the evidence is one thing, but—"

"I don't know, Dallas," Dexter stated abruptly. "And that's what I don't like. I have no idea how far this person would go. But I can't take that chance with you. You're too important to me to risk finding out."

Dallas's eyes misted. "Really, Dexter?"

His eyes locked with hers, then closed. "Of course, you're important to me. Come here."

He drew her into his arms and held her for a moment. Dallas nestled her head onto his wide chest and sighed. He felt so good. And she loved him so much.

"What?"

Dallas raised her head and looked at him. "What?"

He smiled down at her. "You said something, but I didn't understand it."

"Did I?" *Say it,* she told herself. *Tell him you love him.* "Dexter, I—"

It was difficult to talk while being kissed, but Dallas didn't care. Even if she couldn't say it, she could express it.

Pressing herself closer to him, she rose on tiptoe and encircled his neck with her arms. Her fingers toyed with his earlobe, and she felt his arms tighten around her and then loosen, causing her to sway slightly within the circle of his arms.

"What are you doing?" Dexter rasped.

Dallas opened her eyes slowly and looked at him. "Mmm?"

"And why are you looking like that? Why are you suddenly so... aggressive?"

She smiled. "I'm not aggressive, Dexter. I'm just... enjoying myself. Is that bad?"

He frowned. "No... just unexpected—that you'd admit it, that is."

"You don't like it?"

"I like it," he said, eyeing her suspiciously. "What are you up to?"

"Why do I have to be up to something? Do I think you're up to something every time you kiss me?"

He grinned. "Yes. And you're right."

Dallas blushed and pinched him. "Dexter! Can't you be serious for a minute?"

"I'm serious," he insisted, "and I'm seriously positive that if I don't leave now, I'll never leave."

"Dexter, I think we should talk. I have a lot I need to tell you and—"

"I have to leave now," he interrupted quickly. "I have too much on my mind for a serious talk."

Sighing her disappointment, Dallas nodded. "All right. But sooner or later—"

"Good night, sweetheart. I'll call you tomorrow."

"Good night, Dexter," she called as she watched him stride down her front walk. To Dallas it looked as if he was running from her. Why was he so willing to encourage their relationship but so unwilling to say he loved her?

Maybe because he doesn't, a voice inside her head taunted.

Dallas got ready for bed, waging a silent war of emotions. One thing was certain, she decided as she settled into bed. She wasn't going to continue to see Dexter Hudson if he didn't love her. And showing it wasn't going to be enough. Dexter was going to have to tell her. Just as she was going to have to tell Dexter how much she loved him.

*   *   *

When Dexter hadn't called by ten-thirty the next morning, Dallas left her house. She was getting claustrophobic staring at the walls and the telephone. There was no reason why she shouldn't go to the hotel and see him. Maybe she could even help.

The Hotel Hudson was just outside the downtown area on the main thoroughfare. Remembering Dexter's warning about the possibility that whoever had set the fire knew about her doing the audit, Dallas decided to avoid the downtown area altogether and chose the scenic route. It would take her twice as long, but at least she could be reasonably sure no one would see her. Then, if Dexter yelled at her about taking chances, she could tell him how careful she'd been.

She drove north on a state highway for a mile or so, then cut west on a seldom-used county road. When she reached the highway a few miles west, she could go south and park her car behind the hotel without anyone knowing she was there.

Unfortunately Dallas never even got to the highway. Approaching a stop sign at an intersection, she pressed down on the brake pedal, only to feel no resistance. She quickly pumped the brake as she'd done the past couple of times she'd driven the car, but nothing happened.

Looking quickly left and right, she hoped to glide through the intersection without incident. But it wasn't to be.

"Oh, no," she breathed as she saw an old truck bouncing along toward her. The truck had no stop sign and wouldn't see her until it was too late. Holding her breath, Dallas turned her steering wheel to the right and pulled her keys from the ignition.

She hadn't been going more than forty or fifty miles an hour, but it was enough. Cutting the engine's power slowed her down, but not in time to keep her car from plowing into a ditch.

Dallas was prepared for the impact, but was nevertheless pitched forward. Her head struck the steering wheel, although not hard enough to render her unconscious. She just sat in the car for a minute, counting her blessings and wondering what had happened.

"Hey, are you all right?"

She looked over and saw the driver of the truck looking through her window. Dallas nodded.

The man, whom Dallas didn't recognize, opened her door. "You want me to call an ambulance?"

Dallas shook her head. "No. I'm all right."

"What happened? I was going through the intersection and saw you go into the ditch."

Getting out of the car slowly, Dallas turned and retrieved her purse. "I don't really know what happened. I think my brakes failed. They've been feeling a little funny the past day or so, but I hadn't gotten around to having them checked."

The man took her arm to help her up and out of the ditch, but Dallas was already shaking and wasn't too steady on her feet. She slid sideways and fell down, wincing when she felt her wrist twist beneath her.

"Are you all right?"

She struggled back to her feet and let the man practically drag her from the ditch. "I think I sprained my wrist, but—"

"Come on, I'll take you to the hospital."

"No, no," Dallas protested. "It isn't really an emergency. But I would appreciate it if you would take me by my family doctor's office."

Giving him directions, Dallas got into the man's truck and let him drive her to the doctor's office. It probably wasn't a good idea to accept a ride from a strange man, but Dallas didn't think the man, who had to be sixty-five or seventy, posed a real threat. And he had nice eyes. Rubbing her aching temple, she reasoned that most ax murderers probably had nice eyes, too.

Ax murderer or no, the man drove her to her doctor and safely deposited her inside, refusing to take any money for his inconvenience.

Dallas talked to the receptionist, who promised to get her in to see the doctor quickly. During her short wait, Dallas phoned the auto club and asked them to send a tow truck for her car. She was about to call Dexter when the nurse called her name.

Hanging up the receiver, Dallas decided it was just as well. She didn't know what she was going to tell Dexter, anyway. He was going to be angry, she knew, and she didn't particularly feel like listening to him yell at her right then.

Forty-five minutes later, her wrist tightly wrapped, Dallas again approached the telephone. The bump on her head hurt a little, but it wasn't serious. She had some pills for pain, but didn't want to take them yet. Punching out the number of Dexter's office, she barely heard the phone start to ring before it was snatched from its cradle.

"Dallas?"

"Hello, Dex."

"Thank God it's you. I've been crazy for the past hour wondering if something happened to you. I sent someone to your house, but you weren't there. Where are you?"

He sounded so worried that Dallas felt a lump in her throat. "I'm sorry, Dexter. Really, I am. I just wanted to go to the hotel and see you. I thought I could help, but I had an accident and—"

"Accident? Are you all right? Where are you?"

"I'm at my doctor's office on Franklin Street. I'm not really—"

"Don't move. I'll be right there."

"But, Dexter—" Dallas sighed. He'd hung up. She walked back to the waiting room and sat down, cradling her wrist. It was swollen and her fingers looked fat and funny, sticking out of the bandage. She went into the rest room and discovered that having a sprained wrist slowed her down considerably.

Digging into her purse, she found a comb and approached the mirror, intending to comb her hair with her left hand. Seeing the lump on her forehead that had begun to bruise only made her want to cry. She looked absolutely awful, and Dexter was now on his way over to yell at her for not doing what he'd told her. She went back into the waiting room and sat down, still blaming herself for what had happened. It was her fault for not staying at home. None of this would have happened if she'd just—

"Dallas? Sweetheart?"

Dallas looked at him with tear-filled eyes. "I'm sorry, Dex. I know it was my fault, but I—"

"Shh, what is it?" He pulled her into his arms and smoothed her hair. Dallas couldn't stop herself from crying all over his shirtfront and babbling incoherently about what had happened. Dexter couldn't understand a word, but he continued to say he understood and that everything was all right. He led her out to his car when her sobbing subsided, then helped her into the passenger seat. By the time he got behind the wheel, Dallas was wailing again.

"I look so ugly," she moaned, looking at herself in the little mirror on the sun visor.

Dexter flipped the visor up and started the car. "You're beautiful, and you know it."

His brusque statement only set Dallas to sniffling again. Not tearful sobs, but little hiccuping sighs punctuated by loud sniffs. "I know you want to yell at me, so go ahead," she said as they drove toward Dexter's house.

He turned to look at her, genuinely surprised. "I'm not going to yell at you. Why would I do something like that?"

"Because you told me to stay home and I didn't, and look what happened!"

"Oh." He smiled. "Well, as long as you know I was right, why should I yell at you? Don't you think you've been through enough?"

She sniffed again, and he thrust his handkerchief at her. "Yes, I do. And I'm glad you're not going to yell at me, Dex. I don't think I could stand it right now."

They parked in front of Dexter's house a few minutes later, and he helped her into the house.

"It's my wrist that's sprained, Dex, not my ankle."

"Shut up, or I'll carry you."

"Big macho he-man."

"All right."

"Dexter! Put me down."

"No."

"All right, be macho. I didn't feel like walking, anyway."

Mrs. Foley opened the door before Dexter put a foot on the porch. "Oh, my Lord. I thought I heard the car. What happened? No, bring her into the living room."

Dallas managed to tell her story more coherently this time, and with Mrs. Foley and Dexter both helping her, she was lying on the new sectional sofa with her wrist on a pillow within five minutes.

"You mean your brakes just gave out completely?"

Dallas nodded. "Yes. I mean, I thought they felt a little funny yesterday, and I was going to make an appointment to get them checked today, but—"

"What garage did you have them tow it to?"

She gave him the name and address of the garage, and he wrote it down in a little spiral notebook he took from his pocket. "I'll check on your car later and make sure it's repaired."

"Thank you, Dex, but that really isn't necessary. I know the man who owns the garage and I trust him."

Dexter's grim expression didn't alter. "Nevertheless, I'll take care of it."

Dallas was too emotionally exhausted to care. "All right. Whatever. Did your investigator find out anything about the embezzler?"

"Not yet. Does your wrist hurt?"

She nodded. "A little."

"And that knot on your head looks as if it could create a fair headache."

"I guess so."

Dexter sighed. "Did the doctor give you anything for pain?"

"Yes, but, Dexter, I don't really want to take it yet."

He wasn't interested in her reasons. Reaching for her purse, he rummaged around in it until he found the pills. "Here. I don't know why you want to be stubborn about this. It isn't as if you have to drive home."

Dallas swallowed the pills. "Pushy bully."

"Get used to it," he teased. "Now, I want you to get some sleep."

She pouted. "All right. But when I wake up, I want you to tell me everything that's been going on at the hotel."

His warm, firm lips covered hers briefly. "I promise. Now go to sleep."

The muffled ringing of a telephone woke Dallas. Shadows in the room told her it was after sundown, but not yet dark out. Gingerly feeling her head, she noted that although the bump felt bigger, her headache wasn't as bad. Her wrist was uncomfortable, but no longer throbbing.

She cautiously sat up, then stood and made her way to the door. Opening it, she looked out into the hall. There was a light coming from Dexter's den, and the sound of his voice. He must have answered the ringing telephone.

Walking slowly, Dallas paused in the open doorway until Dexter looked up. He motioned for her to enter. "Is that everything so far? Yes, I will. Thanks. See you tomorrow." He looked back up at Dallas after replacing the receiver. "You look better. How do you feel?"

"Better. What time is it?"

"About seven-thirty. Why? Got a date?"

Dallas made a face at him. "As a matter of fact, I do. He's about a hundred and thirty pounds of hungry dog."

Dexter laughed and shook his head. "Not to worry. I imagine you must be hungry, too."

She would have denied it if her stomach hadn't chosen that moment to growl. "Uh, I suppose I am, a little."

Steering her toward the kitchen, Dexter ignored her protests. "I think Morty will understand."

He pushed the swinging door open, and Dallas walked through. Her mouth dropped open when she saw Morty lying on a rug near the door, chewing on a huge steak bone. When he saw her, he jumped up and **ab**andoned his bone to whine and wag his tail at her.

"Hi, guy. What are you doing here?"

"Since he has no comment, I suppose it's up to me to explain," Dexter quipped. "I called your friend Kathy, and she went over to your place and got Morty and packed you a bag and brought them both over."

Dallas turned surprised eyes on Dexter. "Why did you do that?"

"Because I want you here where I can protect you."

"Dexter, I don't think that's necessary. You said yourself that Morty—"

"I've changed my mind," he stated calmly but firmly. "And please don't argue with me. You'd only lose."

Mrs. Foley bustled in then. "Oh, you're awake. Good. I've got dinner all ready. Now you two go and sit down."

After serving the meal, Mrs. Foley retreated to her room. Dallas nibbled on a breadstick.

"What's the matter? Don't you like spaghetti?" Dexter asked.

"I love spaghetti. But right now I want you to explain why you're so determined that I need protecting."

"Oh. Before dinner?" Seeing her arched eyebrow, he shrugged. "Okay. That phone call I just got was from the private investigator. I asked him to stop by the garage tomorrow and see if he can find out what caused your brakes to fail."

"Do you think—"

Dexter held up his hands. "I don't know. I just want it checked into."

The grimness of his expression caused Dallas's throat to go dry. "You think someone may have deliberately—but why?"

"I think that's obvious. Our embezzler could have done it because he found out who you are and what you've been doing at the hotel."

Shaking her head, Dallas tried to gather her thoughts. "But that doesn't make any sense. Why would they want to do something that would garner attention? It isn't as if I'm the only person who's onto them."

"No," Dexter agreed. "But with the fire destroying the hard copies of the records, they probably figured—correctly—that hurting you would take my mind off the hotel, giving them a chance to destroy more evidence."

"What are you going to do?"

Wide shoulders flexed beneath his shirt. "I don't know yet. Jim Lawrence, the private investigator, will be here tomorrow morning to make a report, and I'll talk with him about it. Tonight I just plan to stay here and eat a nice dinner with you, and not talk about the hotel at all."

With that, he turned his attention to his spaghetti, and Dallas started figuring out how she could manage to get him to let her help on the investigation. The sooner it was all over the happier she would be. Because if she was in danger over her involvement, then Dexter was also in danger. And Dallas was just as determined to protect him as he was to protect her.

Chapter Nine

A beam of sunshine slipped between the closed drapes and settled on Dallas's face. She turned away from it with a slight grumble, only to hear a whine and feel a wet nose nuzzling her cheek.

"Morning, Morty," she said, opening her eyes. "No offense, but all things being equal, I'd rather wake up to Dexter's kisses than yours."

Another whine was all she got as an answer.

"I didn't mean that I don't still love you, Mort." Swinging her legs to the floor, Dallas sat up and stretched, looking around the guest room. Gingerly touching the bump on her head, she was relieved to notice that the swelling had gone down. She then flexed her sprained wrist and winced slightly. It wasn't as bad as it had been yesterday, but neither was it healed.

Throckmorton dashed from the bed to the door. Dallas stood and put on her robe. "You'll just have to wait this morning, Morty. I can't go traipsing around Dexter's house half dressed the way I do at home—not yet, anyway."

Walking into the bathroom, she splashed water on her face and brushed her hair. Not being able to do much about the bruise that was performing amazing Technicolor feats on her forehead, Dallas returned to the bedroom and opened the door, admonishing Morty to be quiet as they descended the stairs.

Pushing open the swinging door to the kitchen, she discovered that being quiet wasn't necessary, since Mrs. Foley was making breakfast and Dexter was sitting at the table, drinking coffee and reading the newspaper. They both looked up as she and Morty walked into the room.

"Good morning, Dallas. Did you sleep well?" Mrs. Foley asked.

"Yes, thank you, I did."

Walking between the kitchen counter and the breakfast nook where Dexter sat, Dallas opened the back door and let Morty out. Turning around, she smiled hesitantly at Dexter, wondering why she suddenly felt so shy.

"Good morning." His voice was low and rumbly, and Dallas felt her stomach muscles tighten in response.

"Morning, Dex."

His eyes roamed over her as she sat down at the table. "How's your head?" He brushed her hair aside and studied her bruised skin.

"Better. It looks uglier than it feels. And my wrist doesn't hurt as much, either."

"Good. But the doctor said you should rest and avoid strenuous activity for at least a week."

Dallas's eyes widened. "How do you know what my doctor said?"

He shrugged as he picked up his coffee mug. "I called him."

"Why? I'm perfectly capable of following my doctor's instructions. And I'm surprised he'd tell you anything about my condition at all, since you're not family."

"But since your family is out of town, and you're staying here with me, the doctor was convinced I was the next best thing to family."

Dallas stared at him. She didn't know whether to feel ungrateful for his attentiveness or angry at his presumptuousness. Taking a deep breath, she tried to remain objective, but didn't think it would work.

"Dex, I appreciate the fact that you're thinking about me, but I'm not helpless, and I don't need you to take over my life for me."

Dexter looked surprised. "I wasn't taking over your life. I was just checking to make sure everything was all right."

Sighing heavily, Dallas shook her head. "I know. But why didn't you just ask me what the doctor said?"

"I didn't want to bother you. You were sleeping at the time. Besides, sometimes your stubborn nature takes over, and I didn't want to get a watered-down version of your injuries."

Dallas rearranged her silverware and tried to keep her voice calm. "My stubborn nature? Are you saying that you think I would lie to you about—"

"If it was important enough to you, you would," Dexter finished for her. He folded his paper and set it aside. "Let's be honest, Dallas. You would downplay your injuries if you thought I was worrying too much, wouldn't you?"

Opening her mouth to deny his statement, Dallas found that she couldn't. She probably would try to spare him worrying about her. "Maybe I would," she finally answered grudgingly, "but I'd prefer it if you'd ask me first."

He nodded. "I will. If you'll promise always to tell me the absolute truth when I ask."

Dallas frowned. "That's not fair. Sometimes it's not possible to tell the absolute truth. You have to consider people's feelings and how hearing something might affect them."

"True," he agreed. "But generally speaking, if you promise to be truthful with me, I'll trust you. And you can trust me."

Dallas thought she was probably missing a key element, but nonetheless she nodded. "All right. Just as long as it works both ways. I'm of a curious nature myself, you know.''

His eyes twinkled mischievously as Mrs. Foley came around the counter with their breakfast. "Do I? I'm beginning to think your curiosity will be both the joy and the bane of my existence.''

The private investigator Dexter had hired was due to arrive in an hour, and Dallas was trying to hurry with her shower but finding it difficult with her wrist bandaged.

Feeling slightly rebellious, she unwound the elasticized bandage and stepped under the warm spray. Washing her shoulder-length hair was her most awkward task because she couldn't put any pressure on her sprained wrist.

Turning off the water, she stepped out and dried herself on a huge bath towel before struggling into her white cotton blouse and blue painter pants. After slipping on her blue-and-white sandals, Dallas sat down at the dressing table.

If she put her eye makeup on with her left hand, she'd look like a freak, she decided, so she applied only blush and lip gloss and tried not to notice that she looked sixteen again. Tugging the towel from her head, she managed to comb out her hair, but when she tried to put the bandage back on her wrist, she ran into trouble. She was still trying to get it where she wanted it when she heard a knock on the door.

"Yes?''

The door opened and Dexter poked his head into the room. "What's taking so long? Lawrence will be here in a few— What are you doing?''

Dallas was still struggling with the end of the bandage around her wrist, trying to anchor it. "I'm just putting this bandage back on.''

Walking across the room to stand next to her, Dexter watched for about five seconds, then took over. "Give me that. Why did you take it off?''

Dallas watched as he quickly and expertly wound the bandage around her wrist and hand. "I didn't want to get it wet when I took a shower."

"Why didn't you take a bath?"

"I don't like baths."

"That's because you're just interested in getting clean. One day soon I'll introduce you to 'dirty' bathing."

"Dexter!" Dallas admonished, her cheeks flaming. But she couldn't hide the smile that curved her lips. "Go away. I have to do my hair."

"Sure. How?"

She looked up curiously. Dexter was holding her blow dryer. He looked a little strange to her as she glanced over at the mirror, eyeing the picture they made. "Dexter, get my camera. This is a picture that deserves a place in the Yale alumni magazine."

"You just get wittier and wittier, don't you? Now, I'll hold this and you can hold the brush and we'll—"

"Dex, why don't you just turn it on and point it?"

Ten minutes later Dallas's hair was dry and pulled back into a ponytail. Getting Dexter to tie a ribbon into it hadn't been as difficult as she'd thought. She even thought he looked rather pleased with his efforts as a stylist.

"Dexter? There's someone here to see you," Mrs. Foley called from the hallway, causing two pairs of eyes to lock in the mirror. Dallas looked expectant; Dexter reluctant.

"Please, Dex?"

He groaned and sighed. "I can see that I'm in big trouble." Before she could ask him to elaborate, he said, "All right, you can sit in on the meeting. But that's it. Nothing more."

"Thank you, Dexter," Dallas said primly, walking toward the doorway. Her foot was in the door, she thought as she walked with him down the stairs. She was confident he would come to see things her way before the day was over.

Jim Lawrence was a bland-looking sort of man who, at first glance, seemed utterly relaxed and at ease. It was when

Dallas was introduced to him and looked into his eyes that she understood why he was a good investigator. His eyes were shrewdly assessing and constantly moving.

"Pleased to meet you," he said pleasantly. "I heard you had an accident. Hope you're all right."

"I'm fine," Dallas assured him, sitting on the edge of the sofa.

"What have you found out?" Dexter asked abruptly, sinking down next to her.

Lawrence sat on the window seat, facing Dallas and Dexter. "About the three suspects? Not much. Haven't had enough time yet."

Dexter saw the investigator's gaze settle on Dallas. "What else?"

The man's eyebrows rose, and he looked from Dallas to Dexter, then back to Dallas. "No offense, Miss Shelby, but—" He looked at Dexter. "Is she to be included in all discussions?"

Dallas's head snapped around to see Dexter frowning. If he tried to send her away, she'd kill him. Dexter smiled. "If we tried to get rid of her, she'd just listen at the keyhole."

"Dexter!"

"What? I'm sorry...but try to deny it." Seeing the gleam in her eyes, he quickly turned back to the investigator. "Go on, Jim. Dallas has done most of the work in this thing so far. I see no reason not to let her in on our strategy sessions."

Lawrence shrugged and pulled a small notebook from his jacket pocket. "As I said, I'm still working on tracking down financial and personal information on your three suspects, but I did manage to find out something interesting about Ms. Shelby's accident."

Dallas nodded as calmly as she could. "I see. Was my car badly damaged?"

Lawrence shrugged diffidently. "Depends on how you look at it. It's a little scratched up, and one tire blew when you went into the ditch, but overall the car's in pretty good shape. It was the cause of the accident that I went to check on.''

Dexter's hands were clenched as he looked at the investigator. "What did you find?''

Referring to his notes, Lawrence read the data without inflection. ''There was a small hole in the brake line. Apparently it was too perfect to be caused by a rock or some other natural occurrence.''

Her brow furrowed in confusion, Dallas didn't understand what was being said. ''What does that mean?''

''He's saying that someone purposely punctured your brake line,'' Dexter answered tightly.

Her large green eyes became even larger as realization dawned. Dexter had been right. ''Are you sure?''

''As sure as we can be at this point,'' the investigator stated. ''You see, if the hole had been caused by a rock or a piece of metal, the hole would be jagged or irregular in shape. But this one isn't. It's perfectly round with no rough edges. Probably an ice pick or dart or something like that.''

''But how could anyone do that without being seen? When could they have done it?''

''That's more difficult to tell. Could have been a whole day before the accident. See, the hole wasn't very big. So the brake fluid leaked out gradually, not all at once,'' Lawrence said casually. Listening to his voice, Dallas found it hard to believe they were talking about the fact that someone had tried to kill her—or at least harm her.

Dexter sat grim-faced beside her, alternately contemplating his hands, the floor and his investigator. ''I was afraid of that.''

Knowing Dexter's predisposition, Dallas turned back to Lawrence. ''I know Dexter's opinion on this, but don't you think I should continue to do the audit so that we can find out who—''

''No!''

''Dexter, we can't just wait around. What if they leave town or something?''

"I don't care what they do," Dexter ground out. "As long as they stay away from you."

"You do care," Dallas said gently. "You want to catch them. Now more than ever, if I know you. And I can help."

Dexter shook his head. "No. I can't let you risk it."

"But, Dexter..."

Lawrence cleared his throat. Dallas and Dexter both turned to glare at his interruption. "Sorry," he said dryly, "but I think I have an idea."

"What is it?" Dexter asked cautiously.

"Just hear me out before you say anything. Dallas is right, in a way." At Dallas's pleased smile the investigator sighed. "But finishing the audit could take too much time, as could finishing my investigations of the three suspects. I think it would be in everyone's best interests to accelerate the investigation—at least make the appearance of it."

Dallas frowned, but Dexter nodded. "I think I get what you're saying. We lead them to believe that we have them and let them hang themselves."

Lawrence nodded. "So to speak."

"I don't understand," Dallas admitted. "What are we going to do and—"

"*We* aren't going to do anything. Mr. Lawrence here and I will handle everything."

Dallas felt her frustration level rising again. "Don't get all macho with me, Dexter. I take it that the idea is to get whoever it is to confess."

Lawrence nodded. "That's the idea. The trick is to convince him—or her—that we're onto them, then stand back and watch. Hopefully they'll take the bait."

Worrying the end of her thumb with her teeth, Dallas shook her head. "It sounds sort of iffy. How do we... Wait, I have an idea."

"Uh-oh."

"Be quiet, Dexter. Now whoever punctured my brake line probably also started the fire, right?"

Both men nodded. "That's a safe assumption," Lawrence acknowledged.

"Okay, so it would seem that whoever did it knew that I was working on the audit. They were trying to destroy the evidence and, uh, the person who knew the most about that evidence."

Dexter didn't like her phrasing. "So what? We know they were after you. What's your point?"

"My point is that they think they destroyed the evidence, and they also think I'm no longer working on the audit."

Dexter's frown got deeper, but Lawrence perked up. "Not bad. This could work. We let the embezzler think that some of the evidence was saved and that the little accountant here is still working on it. When your perpetrator tries to get the evidence, you get him."

Dallas and Lawrence both looked at Dexter, waiting. Dallas hoped he wouldn't let his need to protect her interfere with catching the embezzler.

Dexter groaned. "All right, on a few conditions. The main one being that you—" he stared hard at Dallas "—are nowhere near when this thing goes down. And at all other times you're with me. End of discussion," he added when Dallas opened her mouth to protest. She sighed and slumped back into the sofa, a picture of dejection.

Lawrence flicked his amused eyes over his client and his client's accountant. "Okay, now the plan. It has to be simple and logical and unspectacular."

Dexter nodded. "Why don't we just call a meeting, tell them all what's been going on—except that they're the suspects—and ask for their help? We tell them that the only evidence that was saved from the fire was with Dallas and that it's now locked up in my office. Then we wait."

The investigator nodded. "Sounds like it might work. But I think that both of you should be at the meeting."

Dallas sat up straighter and widened her eyes. Maybe she wouldn't be totally left out, after all.

"Why?" Dexter asked.

"Because you don't want the perpetrator to be suspicious of your actions," Lawrence said. "Just laugh off the accident. If anyone asks, say you swerved to avoid a dog or something. Then tell them about the supposed evidence. Let everybody get back to work. I'll wire your office—''

Dallas nudged Dexter in the ribs. ''Why don't you use one of those handy dandy surveillance cameras that worked so well the night your mirror got smashed?''

Dexter smirked. ''I wouldn't think you'd want to be reminded of that night and your blind date.''

''What surveillance cameras?'' The private investigator wasn't interested in their private story, but he was interested in something in their conversation.

Dexter sighed. ''We have surveillance cameras in the hotel for security purposes.''

Jim nodded. ''Maybe we could hook one up. Film is always more damning than tape recordings, you know.''

Dexter shrugged. ''Why not? You could set it up in the burned-out office next to mine, I guess.''

''Good.'' The investigator rose. ''I'll get on it tonight. Hold your meeting tomorrow and we'll start our stakeout tomorrow night.''

Shaking Dexter's hand, the man then nodded at Dallas and left. They remained seated on the sofa for a minute after his departure.

''No, you can't go to the stakeout.''

Dallas pouted on the outside while she fumed on the inside.

The next morning Dallas and Dexter arrived at the hotel together and walked through the lobby to his office. They stopped at his secretary's desk, where Dexter handed the woman a handwritten memo.

''Please type this up and send it to the people I've indicated.''

Barely waiting for the woman's nod, they proceeded to Dexter's office. Once there, they unlocked the doors to the private entrance and the office that Dallas had used.

Seeing the charred walls and furniture for the first time, Dallas shivered.

''Don't think about it,'' Dexter said from the doorway.

Dallas turned to look at him. "It isn't that it happened," she said softly. "It's why it happened. That someone could be so driven to cover up their greed . . . I don't know."

"People have been known to do much worse in the name of greed."

She nodded. "I know. But I've never been personally involved in any of that. I've just read about it or heard about it. It's never really touched me before."

Dexter walked over to her and gently picked up her bandaged wrist, holding it between his hands. "Now do you understand why I don't want you involved in this anymore? It isn't just a paper trail we're following. This person is real and dangerous."

Dallas looked up into his serious face. "I do understand. But I don't think you do. What if I told you that I didn't want you to continue with this investigation because you might be hurt?"

Shaking his head and smiling, Dexter kissed her on her forehead. "I'd say I appreciate your concern, but not to worry."

"But I can't say that to you?"

"It's not the same thing."

Dallas pulled away from him in frustration. "Why isn't it the same thing? Because I'm a woman and unable to cope with a potentially dangerous situation?"

"Dallas, you can argue with me all you like, but it won't change my mind. I'm not letting you put yourself at risk again. You mean too much to me for that."

"Do I?" Dallas asked.

Dexter looked surprised. "Of course, you do. You know that."

Not able to contain herself, Dallas blurted, "All I know is that you care for me and that you say we belong together. But that isn't enough for me. Dexter, I love you. But if you don't—"

The buzzing of the intercom elicited a quiet curse from Dexter as he whirled around and went into his office to speak with his secretary. Dallas quietly followed and waited near the door, wondering why she couldn't have kept her mouth shut.

"They're waiting for us in the conference room," Dexter stated when he straightened away from the desk. Dallas thought he looked uncomfortable. "Jim said he'd set things up while we were in there."

Dallas nodded once. "I know."

"Dallas—"

She shook her head. "No, don't say anything right now, Dexter. You know how I feel—even if I did pick a stupid time to tell you. I've always hoped that you felt the same about me, but you never seem willing to say the words. And until you are, I'd rather not speak about anything else of a personal nature." With that, she opened the door with her left hand and went out, knowing that Dexter was right behind her.

They entered the boardroom together, and Dexter closed the door behind them. He indicated the chair next to his, and Dallas sat down, trying to appear businesslike and professional. The other three people in the room seemed to be curious and, perhaps, a bit apprehensive.

"Sorry about the short notice for this meeting," Dexter said briskly. "But something has come to my attention that I think demands all of your input."

"Something to do with the fire?" Ken Wasserman, seated across from Dallas, asked.

Dexter nodded at his accounts manager. "Yes, it does. But, first, let me introduce all of you to Dallas Shelby. Dallas is a CPA I hired to go over the books in what I thought would be a routine audit."

He introduced each person individually, and Dallas nodded and smiled at each of them. Carl Anderman obviously remembered her from the blind date debacle, but he didn't mention it. Linda Marshall, the day manager, was the other person present, and the next to speak.

"If you don't mind my asking, why did you hire an outside accountant? We usually keep audits in-house—unless there's a problem at tax time, in which case the hotel's tax attorney takes over.''

Dexter nodded. ''I realize that. But, being rather new here myself, I wanted a totally objective opinion. And it's a good thing I did, because Dallas found something that no one here caught.''

The three employees glanced at one another, then at Dallas. Dexter's eyes followed them, but didn't linger on any one person for more than a few seconds.

Dallas cleared her throat and returned their eye contact. ''I began by examining the recent books and working my way backward. As all of you know, that can be a very time-consuming process. I was looking for correct procedure as well as quarterly tallies that balanced.''

''Didn't they?'' Carl Anderman's question was directed at Dexter, but Dallas answered, anyway.

''Yes, they did. That wasn't a problem. What concerned me were some irregularities in the canceled reservations entries.''

Linda Marshall smiled—rather patronizingly, it seemed to Dallas. ''Irregularities in cancelations are to be expected in the hotel business, Ms. Shelby.''

Dallas smiled back at the woman. ''Yes, I realize that. What I should have said was that I noticed regular irregularities.''

''What it comes down to,'' Dexter explained, ''is that someone has been taking money for certain rooms, entering them as cancelations and pocketing the money—except for the cancelation fee.''

Once again the three employees looked at one another and then at Dallas and Dexter. Ken Wasserman cleared his throat. ''How long has this been happening?''

Dexter looked at Dallas and shrugged. ''We don't know. Dallas had just found out the what and the how when the office she'd been working in was doused with gasoline and everything in it was destroyed, including hard copies of many of the records she'd been going over.''

Concerned eyes darted to Dallas. Linda was the one who asked what they were all thinking. "Is that how you hurt your arm?"

"No. I wasn't here at the time of the fire. I sprained my wrist after a minor car accident a couple of days ago. It was my own fault, but at least no one else was involved."

They all nodded sympathetically, then returned their attention to Dexter, who said, "Anyway, the fire destroyed almost all of the evidence Dallas had been able to gather. Therefore, we've decided to ask you three for your assistance."

"Not that I want to appear suspicious," Carl Anderman ventured, "but how can you be sure that one of us isn't the guilty party?"

Dexter shrugged. "I can't be positive, but since you've all worked here more than ten years, I had to go with my instincts...and the instincts of my grandfather, who hired all of you. I'm hoping that with your input, we can resolve this quickly and quietly. And, I assume that if one of you is responsible, that the other two will still work to expose the third. Either way I get to the bottom of it."

Linda Marshall nodded, then frowned. "You said something about some evidence. Did the fire destroy everything?"

Dexter shook his head. "No. Of course, the computer still holds the files, and Dallas will be going back over them, but it will take a while. The only hard copy evidence we have is a stack of readouts from about five years ago that were in my office at the time of the fire. Also, the records from reservations that date before computerization are there. They'll be used in court once we determine who is to be tried. Right now everything is locked in my office. If any of you should come up with anything else, please come to me immediately. If you find any evidence, we'll lock it up with the other things."

"Uh, why haven't you called in the police if you know something's missing?"

Dexter eyed Ken Wasserman and smiled. "The police require evidence. And since the fire, we've had to start rebuilding that base. And we'll do it. It's just a time-consuming operation."

After dismissing everyone with words of caution about secrecy, Dexter and Dallas remained in the conference room.

"Well, what do you think?" he asked.

Dallas sighed. "I don't know. They all look innocent and they all look guilty."

Dexter nodded. "I think we were looking for things in every word or nuance. Well, starting tonight we begin the waiting to find out whether or not it worked."

Nodding noncommittally, Dallas followed Dexter back into his office, where they found Jim Lawrence setting up the surveillance equipment in the burned-out office. He had cut a large hole in the wall to accommodate the camera and was placing a two-way mirror over it. It was a decorative mirror, with small shelves on the sides for knickknacks. It looked normal to Dallas, but she knew that through that mirror Lawrence would be able to record everything that happened in Dexter's office. Including, hopefully, an intruder looking for damning evidence that could be used against him.

"Everything's set up," Lawrence said. "The camera will pick up anything or anyone in the room, even in the dark, because of its infrared capabilities."

Dexter nodded and looked around the office. "I suppose now we wait."

Lawrence nodded. "That's right. I'm going to go out and get some food and coffee for tonight. Also, it wouldn't hurt if you could manage to get a comfortable chair or two for that room. It could be a real long night. I'll be back around five-thirty or so."

Dexter nodded, and as the investigator turned to leave, Dallas stopped him. "Would you mind giving me a lift home? I don't think there's anything left for me to do here today."

When Lawrence looked questioningly at Dexter, he rose and began to offer to take her home himself. Dallas shook her head. "No, that's all right, Dexter. You need to stay here."

He gazed intently at her, then sat back down. "Okay. I'll call you later and let you know what's happening."

Dallas shrugged. She didn't really care anymore about the audit or the stakeout. Dexter had made it pretty clear earlier that he didn't really love her, although he did "care" for her. Dallas didn't think she could build a lifetime commitment on such a lukewarm emotion. "If you like," she finally told him.

She dared to look at him one last time before leaving and saw the hard look in his eyes, the stubborn set of his jaw. So it was better for her just to leave and try to get on with her life. If that were still possible.

Chapter Ten

Dallas wasn't having a great day. After she arrived back home and moped for an hour, she called her father, who was back in town for a couple of days before leaving for another series of towns and dinners and campaign rhetoric. She still didn't feel as comfortable around her father as she wanted, and thought that now was as good a time as any to take another step forward in rebuilding their relationship.

"It's me, Dad."

"Dallas! How are you? Sorry you were on hold for so long, but you know how things are during an election year."

Dallas smiled wanly at the lamp on her end table. "Yes, I know. And I'm fine, Dad, all things considered."

"You know, Marie told me you might be calling. And I confess I wasn't sure if I was looking forward to it or not."

"Why, what did she tell you?"

"That you were in love and that it wasn't going very smoothly."

A wry smile twisted her lips. "That's an understatement."

"Well? Who is he? That Hudson boy? What did he do to you?"

Laughing through the tears that threatened, Dallas said, "Yes, it's Dexter Hudson and he didn't do anything. That's the problem. I love him, but he doesn't love me."

"Oh. I'm sorry, baby. Are you sure?"

Dallas nodded at Throckmorton. "I'm not sure about anything anymore, Dad. I thought he cared—I mean really cared—about me, especially after the accident, but then I told him that I loved him and he didn't say anything. I can't live with that sort—"

"Whoa!" Her father's voice sounded distinctly confused. "What accident?"

Dallas gave her father a brief description of the accident and then lamely updated him on her relationship with Dexter.

"Well, what's wrong with him? Doesn't he know the best girl in New England when he sees her?"

Her father's attempts at cheering her up were unusual to Dallas, but appreciated. "I don't know, Dad. Sometimes I think he's afraid of commitment, then other times I think he's just a Neanderthal who doesn't care."

"Well, I don't know what to tell you, honey. Maybe he just needs a little time. Trusting someone else's love is much more difficult than believing in your own love. You can trust people with your money or your reputation or your career. Even your life. But to trust someone with your heart…that takes a lot of courage. Maybe Dexter needs a little time to adjust and believe and trust in your love."

They talked for a few more minutes, and after she hung up the phone, Dallas wandered out into the backyard with Morty and sat on a lawn chair. What was she supposed to think now? Did Dexter need time? How much time? Could she consign herself to limbo waiting for him?

"Yoo-hoo! Knock knock!"

Dallas looked over her shoulder to see Kathy standing by the gate to the backyard, scratching Morty's ears. "Hi, Kath. Sorry, I guess I didn't hear you."

Kathy proceeded into the backyard. "I guess not. What are you meditating on? As if I didn't know."

Dallas shoved her fingers through her hair. "I'm faced with the dilemma of a lifetime."

"Oh, well, maybe I should've come armed with a cheesecake. This sounds serious."

"It is."

Dallas then explained what had happened, including her surprising but endearing conversation with her father. Kathy nodded and hmmed a few times, but made no comments until Dallas was finished.

"That's a dilemma, all right. From a certain point of view, of course. Yours. From some other girl's point of view there would be no problem at all. She'd grab the hunk and run with him. Haven't you ever heard that actions speak louder than words?"

Dallas blinked at her friend. "What do you mean?"

"Maybe you should think about things from a different perspective. There are a lot of men who tell every girl they go out with that they love her. There's not a whole lot of sincerity out there, you know. It's what they do that proves their feelings. The words are just icing."

Nibbling on her lower lip, Dallas considered Kathy's words.

"Do you think he does love you? Really and honestly?" Kathy prodded.

Dallas hesitated, then smiled. "I think he does."

"So you make him tell you."

"Oh, sure. What do I do, torture it out of him? And what if I'm wrong? I don't think I could stand it."

Kathy shrugged. "So you've got two options—force a confession one way or the other, or forget it and him. I'm sure John Hallett would be thrilled to go out with you again."

"Gag me with a champagne cork. No, seriously, Kathy. Even if I wanted to try to force the issue, I don't think I could. The man is six-three and weighs over two hundred pounds. He pretty much does and says what he wants to."

Kathy's dark eyebrows wiggled mischievously over her blue eyes. "Love is the great equalizer, you know. You've spent time around him. When does he forget to guard his words and feelings?"

"Oh, I get it. The surprise attack. Let's see. Well, I'd have to say when he's scared or angry. He doesn't scare too easily, though. You should have seen him at the doctor's office when he picked me up. He was so sweet."

Kathy nodded. "Yes. But it's meaner to drive someone to fright than to anger."

"I didn't realize there were rules."

"Oh, sure. They're subtle, but they're there."

Dallas sighed. "I don't know. I don't think I'd feel right picking a fight just to manipulate him into saying he loves me. I'd rather hear it of his own free will."

"Then I say continue seeing him and wait. I think he does love you, but he's too stubborn to admit it."

Nodding in agreement, Dallas's hair bobbed against her shoulders. "Stubborn is right. He won't let me in on the stakeout that starts tonight. It might be too dangerous for a helpless female, you know."

"I'm not surprised. Men like to think they're the only ones capable of dealing with real stress. Bunch of sissies. Get them in a department store during a sale and I'll show them stress. You know, regardless of whatever else you do, you shouldn't let him get away with that sort of chauvinism."

Dallas got up and walked toward her back door. "I wouldn't, but considering it *is* his hotel and his investigation..." She jerked the door open and looked back at Kathy. "I really wanted to be in on the end, though."

Kathy followed Dallas into the house and sat down at the kitchen table, watching her friend's face. "You're going to do it, aren't you?"

"Yes, I am. I mean, I just thought of something. Dexter says he couldn't stand it if something happened to me. But what if something happened to him? Who's to say I wouldn't be of some help? I don't want to sit here waiting to find out if something went wrong."

"Not that I'm wishy-washy or anything, but what if something does happen? I mean, could you handle a dangerous situation?"

Dallas nodded. "I think so. If I had to. If Dexter were in danger, I know I could. He's so macho that he thinks he's invincible, so he takes chances he shouldn't."

"What happens when he sees you there?"

"He'll throw me out," Dallas said, deflated. "Unless..."

Kathy leaned forward. "Unless?"

"Unless he doesn't know I'm there."

"Right. What are you going to do—hide?"

"Sure," Dallas stated. "Why not? I'll go over and sneak in the back way and hide. Dexter has a couple of closets in his office for coats and stuff. He won't even know I'm there."

"Uh, being in a closet for several hours might not be the most comfortable thing in the world. What if you get a cramp, or have to go to the bathroom or something?"

Dallas tapped the table. "Good thinking. I'll need to take a cushion to sit on and maybe something to eat. But no liquid. I'll go before I leave."

"I don't mean to sound crass, but when can I write the article about this? I could really use that promotion."

"If all goes well tonight, my journalistic pal, you should be the golden girl at the paper this time tomorrow."

Several hours later Dallas wondered about all the hoopla that traditionally surrounded stakeouts and private detectives. The exciting part—getting into the office and then into the closet without being seen—had taken all of five minutes. The rest of the five hours since her arrival had been spent sitting in that closet, waiting. Even the arrival of Dexter and Jim Lawrence hadn't been enough to alleviate the boredom Dallas was feeling. Nor was it any relief to her muscles, which were getting stiffer by the microsecond.

She'd had to get to the hotel early to avoid being seen by Dexter and Jim. Kathy had driven her over and dropped her off near the rear entrance. Creeping along the hedges behind the hotel, she'd had to hide once from an employee who was heading for the parking lot.

Getting to Dexter's private entrance hadn't been hard, but getting into his office was a little trickier. Knowing that Lawrence wasn't scheduled to arrive until after the night shift came on and Dexter's secretary went home, Dallas and Kathy had had to resort to a rather childish method of getting Dexter out of his office long enough for her to enter through the back door and hide herself in the closet.

In the lobby Kathy had created a minor panic by yelling that she'd just seen a skunk. She'd then hidden in a rest room, coming out to mingle with the crowd of people who were scurrying out of the hotel. Dexter had left his office to see what the commotion was about, and Dallas had entered his office, looked into both empty closets and settled herself in the one farthest from the door.

It had only taken the hotel staff ten minutes to solve the crisis and reassure the guests that it was all a mistake. By the time Dexter had returned to his office, Dallas was in the closet, sitting on her cushion and trying not to breathe too loudly.

Since then, Dexter had left and Lawrence had entered and Dexter had returned. These actions were observed by Dallas through the narrow ventilation slats near the bottom of the closet door. Not that she could see much—just their legs from the knees down, and only when they were within the limited range of her slats.

Looking at the luminous dial of her digital watch, Dallas saw that it was eleven-fifteen. Five minutes later than the last time she'd checked. Her legs were stiff, as well as her bottom, and she'd just about decided that she'd rather be at home watching television. Looking up at the empty clothes bar above her, Dallas decided that if she were very quiet, there was no reason why she couldn't stand up and stretch her muscles. Dexter and Jim were both in the room with the camera—no doubt walking around or sitting on comfortable chairs, she thought jealously.

Slowly, silently, Dallas rose and grasped the clothes bar with her left hand for support when her leg muscles protested. The protests quickly gave way to feelings of relief as her muscles and nerve endings were restored to normal. She sighed quietly and gripped the metal rod tighter and she sagged in an attempt to stretch her back and arm muscles.

Unfortunately the metal bar chose that moment to protest, and a loud squeak erupted from above Dallas's right ear. To her it sounded like a sonic boom, but in reality, she knew it most likely couldn't be heard outside the closet. At least she hoped it couldn't. She was still hoping when the closet door was flung open and she found herself staring into the furious gray eyes of Dexter Hudson.

"Hello, Dexter. Fancy meeting you here."

"What the hell are you doing here?" His voice was a cross between a whisper and a growl, and Dallas swallowed heavily as apprehension flooded her. She didn't think she'd ever seen Dexter quite this angry before.

"I'm here because I think I have a right to be here, to see this thing through. You're not the only one with a stake in this, you know," she whispered indignantly. Holding up her bandaged right hand, she pointed at her bruised forehead. "It's personal with me, too. And not just because of money, either!"

Dexter leaned menacingly into the closet so far that Dallas's back was pressed into the back wall of the closet. "Don't push just to see how far I'll be pushed, Dallas. Now, I want you out of here."

"No."

"Yes."

"I can't. I don't have a car. Kathy dropped me off."

Gray eyes narrowed abruptly. "I don't suppose you happen to know anyone who claimed to have seen a skunk in the lobby earlier today, would you?"

Dallas blinked up at him. "Whatever do you mean, Dexter?"

"That's something else for us to discuss later. And we *will* have a discussion about all of this."

"Right. You mean you'll yell a lot and I'll be expected to say I'm sorry. Forget it. I'm not sorry."

Dexter gripped his head in frustration, then shoved his fingers through his hair. He took a deep breath and clenched his jaw. Dallas knew he was trying to control his anger, but she didn't see why he couldn't see her side of it for once.

"When will you realize that I'm not trying to exclude you?" His voice wasn't as harsh, but neither was it soft. "I'm trying to protect you, and you turn around and throw yourself right back into the middle of it."

Dallas sighed. "Dexter, I just don't see why you have to be so stubborn about this thing. If you'd let me in on it from—"

"*I'm* being stubborn? Got a mirror handy? I'll show you stubborn."

"Very funny, Dex. What are you doing?"

He had stepped back away from her and was shutting the door. "If you want to stay, stay. But this is as far as you go."

With that, he shut the door in her face, and to Dallas's dismay she heard him flip the lock on the other side. Quickly feeling the door panel on her side, she realized there was no lock on the inside. She pressed her face against the wood and whispered as loud as she dared. "Dexter Hudson, unlock this door! You have no right—"

"I have every right. This is my office in my hotel. Now shut up and stop moving around. I'll let you out in the morning if nothing happens."

"Dexter!"

But he was gone, back into the second office, probably to laugh with his stupid private investigator about what an airhead she was. Despicable men. Sitting back down on her cushion, Dallas decided that when he did let her out, he'd be sorry. She'd begun to mentally list all the things she could do to him when she heard a scraping sound, and then the sound of a door opening. If it was Dexter coming back to— no, it wasn't Dexter, she thought suddenly. Because it wasn't the door in the wall to the right of her that opened. It was the door to the hotel.

Dallas's breath caught in her throat. It was the person they'd been waiting for. Leaning forward on her knees, she looked through the slats of the ventilator. The weak rays from the moon coming through the window weren't enough for her to make out anything but shadows. Then a flashlight clicked on, its beam hitting the floor.

Through the slats Dallas could see the beam of light and the legs of the man walking toward Dexter's desk, where he started rummaging through the drawers. Not finding what he was looking for, he proceeded to the file cabinet next to it and opened it with a key. Dallas wondered why Dexter's employees had keys to his office and his file cabinet.

Leaving the file cabinet, the man walked to the center of the room and stood there. Dallas wondered what Dexter and Lawrence were waiting for.

It was then that the man lowered his hand into Dallas's line of vision. In it was a gun, its dull metal finish gleaming menacingly in the dim light. Then she saw the beam from the flashlight sweeping over the walls. It landed on the door to the office where Dexter and Jim were. Dallas felt her heart leap into her throat. What if they weren't armed? Did private investigators carry weapons? The ones she saw on television did . . . but she'd never seen Jim with one.

Fear gripped her more tightly when she saw the man walking toward the adjoining office door. When he suddenly stopped, she was afraid he'd heard the pounding of her heart.

The beam from his flashlight flicked around the room. When it suddenly struck and lingered on her ventilation slats, Dallas had to fight to keep the gasp from escaping her throat.

The legs were walking toward her then, following the beam of light that was centered on the closet door. When the doorknob rattled, Dallas jerked backward and abruptly felt the wall against her back. Never having considered herself a claustrophobic person, she was rapidly changing her mind. The closet's dimensions had suddenly become much smaller.

With her eyes riveted on the doorknob, knowing it was about to turn and the door would open, Dallas held her breath, having no idea what she was going to do when confronted with a man with a gun pointed at her.

She didn't have the opportunity to find out, because just then she heard Dexter's voice.

"Hold it right there, Carl."

Carl? Carl Anderman, Dallas thought. She had never liked him, from the first time she'd been summarily brought before his sour presence. But her thoughts about who it was were instantly supplanted by what he was and what he was capable of. She knew it would be senseless to yell a warning since Dexter had no doubt been watching for the past several minutes.

"Put the gun down. My friend here is probably a much better shot than you, anyway."

Dallas didn't see why Dexter was taking such unnecessary chances. Even if Lawrence did have a gun, Dexter shouldn't be exposing himself to harm like that. It was crazy.

A short laugh, really more of a snort erupted from Carl Anderman. Dallas scooted back to the slats, where she watched the legs of three men in frustration. "I should have known it was a setup," the night manager said. "There isn't any evidence in here, is there?"

"No, there isn't," Dexter said, his voice controlled, but Dallas could detect the threads of anger that he was holding in check. "There's no evidence, but then we don't need any now, do we? Your being here is enough for us. It'll be relatively easy to trace the stolen money to you now. I don't suppose you'd like to tell me why you stole from my grandfather for all those years, would you?"

"No, I wouldn't. I don't think you'd really get it. He didn't. And he was never suspicious, either. He's the one who gave me a copy of the keys to this office. I was a trusted employee. And besides, what harm did it do? He never missed any of it. Rich people like you Hudsons never will understand. Why should you get everything and people like me get nothing? I was just evening things up a bit.''

"Quite a justification, Carl, but I don't think a judge and jury will buy it.''

"No, probably not,'' Anderman said bitterly. "I was planning on leaving town when you brought in your little auditor. If it hadn't been for her, I'd have been gone and nobody would have been the wiser.''

Dexter's legs shifted a step closer toward the embezzler. "Is that why you punctured her brake line, so you could buy yourself some time?''

"I saw her here late one night, leaving by that back door. I thought she was just your girlfriend, like everyone else did. After that I paid closer attention and figured out that an audit was being done on the sly. I just needed some more time to set up my unexpected 'vacation.' ''

"Well, now you can expect to spend your vacation right here in New Hampshire, but I don't think it's a place you'd have chosen.''

Dallas saw Anderman's feet sidestepping, and struggled to keep them in view. What was he planning?

Suddenly Anderman's legs darted to the side, and Dexter and Lawrence started forward. The back door was flung open by Anderman but, instead of leaving, Anderman backed into the office. Then Dallas saw two more pairs of legs. Security!

"Give me the gun, Mr. Anderman,'' one of the guards said.

"I want to see my lawyer,'' the night manager grumbled.

Dallas stood up, no longer terrified that someone would get hurt. She knocked on the door. "Dexter? Let me out.''

"You'll need a lawyer, Anderman,'' Dexter said. "But right now you're going to go down to the police station.''

"Dexter!'' Dallas pounded this time. "It's over. Let me out!'' She rattled the doorknob for emphasis, but didn't hear any response.

He jerked the door open just as she was drawing back to pound on it, and Dallas fell out of the closet, her fist hitting his solid chest. "I might have known you'd turn violent," he said.

Looking hastily around the office, Dallas saw that the security guards were leaving with Carl Anderman in tow. Jim Lawrence saluted them both in a lazy fashion and grinned at Dexter as he left. "Maybe you shouldn't have let her out."

"I probably shouldn't have," Dexter agreed. "A little meditation time on the evils of impulsiveness might have done her some good."

Then Lawrence was gone and they were alone. Pushing past him, she put a few feet of space between them so that it wouldn't hurt her neck to look up at him.

"I wouldn't think that I was the only one in need of a little meditation on rash acts. What did you think you were doing confronting Anderman without a gun?"

"How do you know I didn't have a gun?"

"Did you?"

He hesitated, then shook his head. "No, but Jim did."

Dallas's green eyes flared. Now that she was no longer frightened for his safety, she could release her emotions. "So I guess that if he'd shot you, Jim could've shot him and everything would have been all right!"

"That didn't happen."

"No, but it could have."

Dexter leaned toward her challengingly. "It was more likely that he would have shot you if he'd opened that closet door."

They stood staring at each other defiantly. Then Dallas felt herself starting to shake. Forcing herself not to collapse from sheer relief that it was all over, she clenched her fists. "Do you have any idea how scared I was when I saw him heading toward the door with that gun?"

Dexter's eyes widened briefly. "Yes, as a matter of fact I do. I was feeling that and more when he suddenly stopped and started toward that stupid closet."

"So you had to charge out and challenge him?"

"What did you want me to do? Let him find you?"

"What if he'd shot you?"

"At least he wouldn't have shot you!"

Dallas stared into his turbulent eyes for another second, then suddenly flew against his body, holding him tightly. "Don't you ever do anything like that again, Dexter Hudson. I couldn't stand it."

His arms went around her slowly, and then tightened as his cheek came down to rest on the top of her head. "I'll do it again in a minute if you're in danger. So if you want me to stay out of trouble, you stay out of trouble. I think my hair's gone white."

Dallas pulled back so that she could look at him. "Were you really frightened for me, Dexter?"

"What kind of stupid question is that? Of course I was. I was afraid I wouldn't ever..."

His voice trailed off, but his eyes remained intent on her upturned face. Dallas smoothed her hand along his back. "Afraid you wouldn't ever... what?"

Large hands cradled her face. "I was afraid I wouldn't get the chance to tell you how much I love you."

Her breath caught in her throat, but Dallas managed to whisper, "Really?"

He nodded once before his lips covered hers in a kiss so tender yet so passionate that Dallas felt tears pricking her eyelids. Then she was suddenly airborne as Dexter swept her up into his arms, carried her over to the leather sofa and sat down. "Yes, I admit it. I do love you. And I want you to marry me. You will, won't you?"

Dallas nodded, oblivious to the tears that were threatening to spill down her cheeks. "Yes. What took you so long?"

The ensuing pause was so long that Dallas leaned forward and kissed him gently, urging him to talk to her. Finally he shrugged. "I was afraid that you really didn't love me. I knew you were attracted to me, though, and I figured that if I could keep you close to me, you'd fall in love with me eventually. When you said you loved me, I was so shocked that I couldn't say anything. Then we had to go to that damn meeting. After that you wouldn't listen to me and left. I couldn't wait for this whole mess to be over with so that I could find you and set everything straight.''

Dallas groaned and shook her head in mock despair. ''My dad said you might have been afraid. He said some people are afraid to trust someone else with their heart.''

''I guess I was. I didn't have very good role models growing up. None, in fact, except for my grandfather.'' He paused and looked at her curiously. ''Your dad told you this? When did you talk to him?''

Dallas toyed with a button on Dexter's shirt. ''Earlier today. And I had a nice talk with him at the house a few days ago. He's not the person I thought he was, you know. He was . . . different. Warmer, I think.''

''That's good. Now maybe we can work on my parents.''

She settled her head on his shoulder. ''We will. I have a plan.''

''Uh-oh.''

''Don't worry, Dexter. I'll take care of everything.''

''That's what I'm afraid of. Have you always been a schemer?''

Dallas nodded against his shoulder. ''Yes, I suppose so. If you hadn't been such a macho jerk when we first met, I'd have schemed for you then. But you were always so mean to me. Well, almost always. Then you left me and broke my heart.''

''I did?''

''Yes. I'd lost so much that I'd loved. My mother was dead, my father was always gone, and then you. I only had Freelance, and then I had to give him up. But after I moved back to Concord, things started looking better. I had my own business, and I had Kathy and Morty. And then, when you moved back to town, I was afraid you'd make me love you again and leave again. Then I wondered if you'd even remember me at all.''

"Oh, I remembered a lot. I remembered that if you hadn't been so young that I wouldn't have wasted so much time that summer."

"Really? I thought you thought I was a brat."

"You were," he affirmed, and she playfully punched him in the arm. "You still are. But I guess I like brats. Even then you were more interesting than any of the other girls I knew. Except for...uh..."

Dallas blushed. "Yes, well. Now that we're getting married, you'll have my interesting mind as well as...uh..."

They both laughed and Dexter squeezed her tightly. "I may love you, but that doesn't mean I won't still be overprotective of you. I'll probably be worse. Just thought I'd warn you."

"That's all right," she sighed. "I'm getting used to it. Just don't get chauvinistic and we'll be all right."

"I'll try, but one thing is definite—no more harebrained schemes with Kamikaze Kathy. I can't afford to replace that mirror every time—"

"I did *not* break that mirror," Dallas cried indignantly. "It was John Hallett, that creep. If he hadn't—"

"I know," Dexter cut in. "And I thanked him personally for it."

Green eyes blinked in confusion. "What do you mean, you thanked him?"

Dexter shrugged and looked at her warily. "I located him about four days after you started work on the audit."

"You did?" Her lips twitched with laughter. "It took Kathy and me almost a week to find him."

They stared at each other for a moment, then broke out laughing.

"So, when are you going to marry me, San Antonio?"

Dallas smiled at him through watery eyes. "Anytime you say."

He kissed her gently and smiled. "I never thought you'd be so compliant."

"Enjoy it while you can. It might not last long."

"How long do you think I have?"

Dallas placed her good hand behind his neck and pulled. "Not long if you don't kiss me."

He laughed. "I guess I can be compliant, too. But only for something important." His eyes twinkled. "Say, if I wanted to open a bottle of champagne and celebrate, you wouldn't throw it at me, would you?"

"Only if you don't kiss me . . . right now."

Epilogue

It had been a wonderful month for Mr. and Mrs. Dexter Hudson. They had had a beautiful wedding in Concord, attended by everyone in the county, followed by a glorious two-week honeymoon in Hawaii, over which the bride was still occasionally blushing.

Now, back at the big house on the outskirts of town, the newlyweds were enjoying an "après honeymoon" with little regard for work or their notoriety, following a newspaper story written by a friend of the bride about embezzlement at the groom's hotel.

On this particular late summer day, Concord's newest married couple was swimming and relaxing with their friend and housekeeper. Assorted pets were also present.

Mrs. Foley sat under the umbrellaed table, reading a detective novel and smiling at them indulgently. Throckmorton was sleeping in the sun, uninterested in the people swimming laps in the pool. Lady Macbeth was batting a piece of paper around the yard near the hedge.

Dallas had decided that she must be a latent lecher. Every time she looked at Dexter, she wanted to jump on him and kiss him. And a few other things. She smiled to herself and pushed off the end of the pool to begin another lap. Married life was . . . well, pretty wonderful.

She stopped when she reached the other end of the pool. She had finished ten laps and that was enough. She rested her arms on the side of the pool and let her breathing return to normal. Throckmorton was just in front of her, sleeping in the sun. She flicked water at him, laughing when he shook his big head and looked at her accusingly.

"Sorry, Morty, I just couldn't resist. I know I'm a mean, untrustworthy person, and you should probably never speak to me again."

Mrs. Foley chuckled but didn't say anything. Dallas smiled at her, then back at Morty, who had risen and was walking toward her, his long tail wagging.

"Aw, you're such a pal, Mort," she said, scratching him behind his ears. "You know I still love you."

Suddenly her waist was encircled by a large arm and her neck was nuzzled. Dexter held the side of the pool with his free hand and whispered against her neck, "As long as you love your husband more than your dog, he can stay."

Dallas laughed and turned in his arms, looping hers around his neck. "I think you're safe. Morty's nice, but he's lacking certain qualities I find very . . . stimulating in a husband."

He smiled and kissed her lingeringly. Finally he pulled back and smiled. Then he slipped down into the water, his head disappearing within the circle of her arms.

Dallas paused, treading water for a moment, looking around for Dexter, then saw him, touching the bottom of the pool and pushing upward. A second before he touched her she knew his intent and screamed.

His hands grasped her waist and tossed her into the air. She flailed helplessly, laughing before she hit the water. When she surfaced, she glanced around for Dexter and saw him swimming toward her. Throckmorton was barking and running up and down the side of the pool.

She turned onto her back and paddled her feet hard, causing a wake and splashing water into Dexter's face. She realized this was a tactical error when he grasped one of her ankles.

Dallas stopped and held her breath, certain he was going to jerk her underwater. She felt his hand slide along her leg under the water, and when it reached her thigh, she pulled her leg back.

"Dexter..." She gestured towards Mrs. Foley, sitting poolside. When he glanced over at his housekeeper, his grip loosened and Dallas spun away, splashing water into his surprised face. He struck out in a powerful freestyle after her, and Dallas shrieked, looking around for a quick exit. She took evasive action, swimming in the opposite direction, right by Throckmorton, who was running up and down, barking wildly, and Dallas understood from the tone of his growls and barks that he wasn't playing. He thought Dexter was threatening her.

Just as she opened her mouth to reassure Morty, Dexter grabbed her by the waist and pulled her next to him, and the two of them started sinking underwater together.

"No...wait...Dexter!"

Suddenly, with wide green eyes, Dallas saw a blur of black fur flying through the air and landing in the water with a great splash. Dexter's voice was almost hushed when Morty hit the water.

"Wow, I didn't know he could do that."

"Dexter! Come on."

Dallas had already reached her waterlogged hound, who no longer looked fierce and protective. Now Morty looked pathetic and helpless as he paddled around, holding his frightened eyes above the surface of the water.

"Don't worry, baby," she soothed. "Mama and Daddy will help you get out of this nasty old water."

"I'll have you know there's nothing the least bit nasty about this water. And this hound is hardly my idea of acceptable offspring."

"Dexter, save the cracks. Morty is in trouble. Look at his eyes. He's so scared."

As they struggled to push the huge dog to the edge of the pool, Mrs. Foley had grabbed a few towels and was waiting for them near the stainless-steel ladder in the shallow end of the pool.

Dexter stood in waist-deep water, his arms around the struggling body of Throckmorton. "Now what? He's taller than you. Why doesn't he just jump out?"

"Because he's too scared. I can tell. Look at him."

Dallas climbed out of the pool and knelt on one of the towels Mrs. Foley had fetched. She reached out for Morty's front paws. "I'll hold his front and you push him up from the back."

"Oh, sure, just heave-ho. How much does this horse weigh, anyway?"

"I'm sure you've bench-pressed more, Mr. Muscle—now shove!"

He shoved, but a wet dog could be pretty slippery. "The weights I bench-pressed didn't move around," he gasped.

With Dallas pulling and Dexter pushing and Mrs. Foley offering strategic advice, they managed to get Throckmorton out of the pool. He knocked Dallas down and licked her face in gratitude, then proceeded to shake and spray water over everything within a thirty-foot radius.

Dallas laughed. "Thank you, Morty. Now we don't have to take a shower."

Mrs. Foley chased the dog with a towel, saying something about a proper bath, and they disappeared around a hedge, the kitten trying valiantly to catch up with them. Dexter heaved himself out of the water and sat on the edge of the pool, regarding Dallas's prone body. "You know, I could have sworn you made a crack about my muscles just a minute ago."

Dallas sat up warily. "Did I? Oh, I don't think so, Dex. You see, I have nothing but admiration for your muscles."

He turned and knelt next to her. "No, I distinctly remember being referred to as Mr. Muscle. That sounded derogatory to me."

Dallas didn't know what he was up to, but it didn't sound dry. She was about to take evasive action when she heard the rattle of a truck beyond the hedge on the road that led to the stable.

Dexter looked over her shoulder with a smile on his lips. "Right on time. Come on. Put on your shoes."

Dallas frowned in confusion but accepted his outstretched hand and rose, sliding her feet into thongs and reaching for her terry-cloth wrap. Dexter slipped on his laceless sneakers and draped a towel around his neck. Then they walked around the hedge and saw the groom getting out of a truck, which was pulling a horse trailer.

Dallas's eyes widened. "You bought another horse? Why didn't you tell me?"

Wide shoulders lifted and fell. "It was a surprise. A wedding present."

"But you already gave me this," she said, raising her hand and showing him her wedding and engagement rings, their several diamonds twinkling brightly.

Dexter kissed her fingers. "I know. But this is extra."

The groom had opened the gate and entered the trailer and was slowly backing the horse down the ramp to the ground. A blanket covered most of his body, but when she saw his head, Dallas gasped. "Freelance!" Running forward, she took the rope of the halter from the groom and looked into the eyes of her old friend. "Oh, Freelance, sweetie, it's really you."

The horse's ears twitched, and he nudged Dallas's shoulder with his velvety snout. Tears ran heedlessly down her cheeks as she flung her arms around his neck. "I missed you so much," she whispered to the Arabian, who nudged her again.

Stepping away, Dallas turned and looked at Dexter, who was grinning and looking as if he'd swallowed not only a canary but a whole ostrich. Walking up to him, Dallas turned her tear-stained face up to his and grasped his hands in hers. "I didn't think it was possible," she whispered.

"What," he teased, "that you'd ever see that horse again?"

Dallas shook her head. "No. After everything that's happened, our wedding and our honeymoon and everything...I didn't think it was possible to love you more than I did. But I do."

She thought she saw the sparkle of tears in his eyes but was engulfed in his embrace too quickly to be sure. Then she heard his hoarse whisper in her ear.

"That's what makes our love so special. It has no bounds. It's free to grow deeper every day. And it will. I promise."

* * * * *

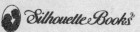

Silhouette Special Edition

proudly hails

WOMEN OF GLORY

from Lindsay McKenna

Soar with Dana Coulter, Molly Rutledge and Maggie Donovan—
Lindsay McKenna's WOMEN OF GLORY. On land, sea or air, these
three Annapolis grads challenge danger head-on, risking life and limb
for the glory of their country—and for the men they love!

May: NO QUARTER GIVEN (SE #667) Dana Coulter is on the brink
of achieving her lifelong dream of flying—and of meeting the man who
would love to take her to new heights!

June: THE GAUNTLET (SE #673) Molly Rutledge is determined
to excel on her own merit, but Captain Cameron Sinclair is equally
determined to take gentle Molly under his wing....

July: UNDER FIRE (SE #679) Indomitable Maggie never thought
her career—or her heart—would come under fire. But all that changes
when she teams up with Lieutenant Wes Bishop!

A Lasting Love

The passionate Cancer man is destined for love this July in Val Whisenand's FOR ETERNITY, the latest in our compelling WRITTEN IN THE STARS series.

Sexy Adam Gaines couldn't explain the eerie sense of familiarity that arose each time his eyes met Kate Faraday's. But Mexico's steamy jungles were giving the star-crossed lovers another chance to make their love last for all eternity....

FOR ETERNITY by Val Whisenand is coming this July from Silhouette Romance. It's WRITTEN IN THE STARS!